PROJECT XCALIBUR

GREG PACE

G. P. PUTNAM'S SONS
AN IMPRINT OF PENGUIN GROUP (USA) INC.

G. P. PUTNAM'S SONS
An imprint of Penguin Young Readers Group
Published by The Penguin Group
Penguin Group (USA) Inc., 375 Hudson Street, New York, NY 10014, USA

USA | Canada | UK | Ireland | Australia | New Zealand | India | South Africa | China
Penguin Books Ltd, Registered Offices: 80 Strand, London WC2R 0RL, England
For more information about the Penguin Group, visit penguin.com

Library of Congress Cataloging-in-Publication Data is available upon request.

Published simultaneously in Canada. Printed in the United States of America.
ISBN 978-0-399-25706-3
1 3 5 7 9 10 8 6 4 2

Design by Ryan Thomann. Text set in Palatino.
Lightning bolt image courtesy of Etienne du Preez/Shutterstock.

ALWAYS LEARNING   PEARSON

For Abby.
Dream big.

1

161:42:09

I HAD MOTOR OIL in my eyes, and it stung.

Luckily I knew the underside of a pickup truck like the back of my hand, so finishing the oil filter change with my eyes closed was no biggie. I dug the heels of my sneakers into the dirt and slid closer to the empty filter housing. With the truck an inch above my face and every tiny pebble beneath me digging into my back, wiping my eyes wasn't an option. I blindly grabbed the new oil filter, swept my arm out to my side, then brought it around to twist the filter into place. Even with my eyes on fire I grinned: I was that much closer to fifteen bucks.

I slid out from under the truck and opened my eyes. They still burned, but my hazy view wasn't a problem; I also knew my town and everything in it like the back of my hand. Thing is, that wasn't really something to brag about, considering Breakwater was about as un-special as a place can be: a one-bowling-alley, one-movie-theater (with *one* screen) town. We didn't have tumbleweeds blowing through the streets, but it wasn't Manhattan, either.

I turned and hurried through the back door of the diner where Mom worked, my eyes brimming with hot tears as I barreled through the kitchen.

"Hey, Ben—what's shakin'?" Denny, the diner's owner and cook, chirped as the door slammed behind me. He was cooking up his specialty, a greasy culinary monstrosity he affectionately called "The Mess."

Denny let me use the lot behind his diner as an auto workshop whenever I needed it, probably because Mom was the best waitress he had and he wanted to keep her happy. "Gotta wash my eyes," I blurted. I stumbled into the bathroom and jammed my elbow against the light switch. The overhead fluorescents flickered, illuminating pale green stained with decades of airborne cooking grease.

I leaned over the tiny sink. Even the water felt greasy on my skin, but pretty much all the water in Breakwater felt that way, as if the town only got the stuff that nobody in Dallas or Houston wanted.

I scrubbed my eyes and, as my world finally came into focus, looked at myself in the mirror. I didn't look much like my parents. My dad had been a firefighter, but he'd died almost a year ago, when I was twelve, so it was just me and Mom. Sometimes I got angry at him for leaving us like he did, but he was just doing his job, and doing it *well.* He really deserved the last name Stone. He was tall and strong, with shoulders like the top ledge of a brick wall. I often wondered if there was any way I'd "blossom" (Mom's word, not mine) into a man like he was. But honestly, the last word that came to mind when looking at me was "Stone." *Styrofoam*, maybe.

I turned to leave, but before I could make it out, the door on the bathroom's one stall swung open. A small boy stared up at me.

"Greetings," he said with a smile.

He looked about eight years old. He wore a checkered short-sleeved shirt buttoned all the way up, a fishing hat, and bulky cargo shorts. Black socks poked out of his white sneakers. Total dork.

I gave him a quick nod. I had more important things to worry about, like collecting fifteen bucks from Todd Byers, who was supposed to be waiting inside the diner for me.

"You okay?" I asked.

He nodded. "Splendid, Benjamin."

"Do I know you?"

"Not yet, you don't."

My eyes narrowed. He was *weird*, and I wasn't in the mood for games. I probably should have turned and left, but that didn't feel right. I grabbed his hand.

"C'mon. I'll get you back to your folks."

It was the Sunday dinner rush: lots of clanking utensils, talking, and chewing. The twelve booths (six along each side wall) were jammed full of kids wearing baseball

3

or football uniforms, celebrating weekend victories or drowning their losses in boatloads of shakes and ice cream. This kid didn't belong with any of them. For one thing, he wasn't wearing a uniform, and for another, he didn't look very athletic to me (unless you consider fishing a sport, which I don't).

I spotted Mom darting around the cluster of tables in the center of the diner. She had plates of food balanced on her arms, and gave me a wink as she passed.

"Which ones are your parents?" I asked the kid, yelling over the noise. He didn't answer.

I scanned the diner, but didn't see a set of anxious parents or Todd anywhere. I leaned down. "Look, dude—I want to help you, but I gotta collect money for a job. It's kind of important."

"My parents aren't here," he said calmly. "I can assure you of that."

I wasn't this kid's babysitter. But I couldn't leave him, and I couldn't afford to stand there for two minutes. I grabbed his hand again and maneuvered around the crowded tables. I finally spotted Todd wedged into a corner table with his friends up at the front.

Todd's parents owned one of the biggest wheat farms in Texas. Apparently, working on a farm does wonders for muscle tone, because Todd was built like a Transformer, which made him the king of middle school football. On top of that, he *drove*. You could legally get a license at fourteen if you worked on a farm—of course, you were only supposed to drive farming vehicles, and only within a half-mile radius of the farm. But Todd never paid attention to the rules, and no one ever gave him trouble.

He spotted me as I approached. "You done with my truck yet, Stone?" he barked, scrunching his cinder block–shaped face.

I held up a finger and hurried out front with the kid.

"Do you see your folks?" I pressed. "Or their car?"

The kid turned to me, and for the first time, I got a good look at his face under that hat. He was pasty pale, and since everyone around here was always sunburned, I knew the little guy wasn't from Breakwater. And there was something about his eyes that bugged me. They were . . . creepy somehow.

"I need your assistance, Benjamin," he said, straightening and crossing his arms. His little face was strangely determined.

"Yeah. That's what I'm trying to—"

"No. I appreciate your concern for my well-being. In fact, I anticipated it. And it's commendable that you've taken it upon yourself to earn money at this young age."

Commendable? My young age? I was at least five years older than he was! The kid was definitely a hoop shy of a basketball court.

"I'm saying that we *all* need your assistance. Urgently."

"All who?" I squinted against the sun beaming off the jumble of cars in the lot.

He spoke softly, leaning close. "Mankind."

I grabbed his hand again. "If you don't want my help, then I'll get Denny to call Sheriff Tulley. *He* can find your folks. What's your name, anyway?"

I glanced into the diner windows. Todd and his buddies weren't at their table anymore. *Not* good. I'd left Todd's keys on the seat of his truck.

My stomach sank. I rushed back into the diner, turning to the kid as I went.

"Listen, stay right here until I—"

But the kid was gone now, too. *Fast little bugger. Maybe he's athletic after all.*

"*Really* not good," I seethed, then slalomed around the crowded tables, through the kitchen, and blasted out back to find Todd and his buddies already in his truck with the engine rumbling.

"Wait!" I shouted, running with all I had. "When are you going to pay me for the oil change?!"

Todd sneered: He'd pay me when bacon flies. He gunned the gas and surged past me, so close I had to jump out of the way. I ended up on my butt, coughing through his exhaust. As I sat there and watched his truck barrel away, I thought of Dad. Sometimes, when I missed him more than usual, Mom would say not to worry because *Your father is always with you, always watching.*

I wondered what Dad would think of me sitting in a cloud of dirt and truck exhaust. Would he be disappointed? If *I* was a bona fide hero, I'd sure as heck be disappointed in a son who couldn't even collect fifteen bucks from a meathead like Todd Byers.

The back door of the diner opened and Denny came out, holding two trash bags. He stopped halfway to the Dumpster when he saw me.

His brow furrowed. "You okay, Benny-boy?"

"Awesome," I replied blankly.

Denny tossed the garbage and plodded back inside. A few moments later, Mom emerged. I got up and dusted myself off as she walked over.

"Everything alright, honey?"

"Todd left without paying me for an oil change, that's all. I'll get it from him at school." I tried to sound casual.

Mom reached out and brushed some of the dirt off my shoulders. "Are you heading home now?"

I nodded. If I said much more, she might have heard the disappointment in my voice, and I didn't want her worrying.

"I'll see you after my shift," she said, forcing a tiny smile. "I'll make a late dinner, then we'll watch some TV?"

"Okay, Mom."

I swallowed hard. She put her hand under my chin and tilted my head up. Sometimes I swear she could read my mind.

"I love you, honey."

"Love you too, Mom."

I gathered my tools and put them in my rusty toolbox,

then walked around the side of the diner. My thoughts turned to what that weird little kid had said.

We all need you. Urgently.

All who?

Mankind.

"What a little nut-job," I muttered.

2

144:19:57

"SINCE ARTHUR WAS ABLE to pull Excalibur from the stone, he was destined to wield the fabled sword and be king. After that he was invincible, especially with Merlin, the greatest wizard in history, at his side."

I looked up from my paper.

"Thank you, Ben," said my Reading Lit teacher, Mr. Ellington, turning to the rest of the class. "Any questions for Mr. Stone?"

I tensed. A Monday that began with me standing at the front of a classroom giving an oral book report was about as enjoyable as a trip to the dentist. Good thing I knew all the stories about King Arthur, Excalibur, and the knights of the Round Table inside out, since Dad used to tell them to me before bed.

Mr. Ellington was a very large guy who always wore bow ties and heinous sweater vests (even in summer), and I hated his assignments. But when he announced that we'd be giving a speech about one of the books on his reading list, I was thrilled to find out that *The Once and Future King* was about King Arthur. I didn't even know there *were* books about King Arthur and Excalibur. I thought Dad just made up those stories each night.

A hand went up. It was Chad "The Dorf" Dorfler, a splotchy-cheeked kid who wore bulky black eyeglass frames because he thought they looked "hip," when they just made him look like a young Mr. Potato Head.

"How come only Arthur could pull out the sword? What was so special about him?" He gave me a little grin. He and I were friends, but he loved making me squirm.

"He . . . just had what it takes to be a hero," I explained.

Hero. That word was used to describe Dad a lot after he died.

"Cool," The Dorf said, accepting my tepid answer. When nobody else raised a hand, Mr. Ellington nodded my dismissal. As I walked back to my desk, Kimberly Wexler smiled at me, then she and her BFF, Madison Bryant, giggled in that way that girls do sometimes. I've always been a little confused by that giggle. Were they laughing *at* me?

"Kim and Madison are totally into you," The Dorf whispered with a pump of his eyebrows as I sat down. "Probably wanna have your babies."

I rolled my eyes. Kimberly and Madison were two of the prettiest girls in school. Plus, I was reluctant to believe anything that came from a kid who *wanted* to be called The Dorf.

After Reading Lit, it was time for gym, a torture-fest run by Coach Denton. Denton was tall and lanky and thought he could make his muscles look bigger by sporting skintight stretchy shirts.

"Circle up!" He drew circles in the air and pointed *up* to the ceiling. "Big day today!"

We were about to be subjected to one of his legendary obstacle courses. There'd be lots of crawling (in gym shorts, on a hard-as-nails basketball court floor), jumping, and, worst of all, the most heinous activity ever invented—climbing a rope to the gym ceiling. I don't know what genius came up with the idea of making kids clamber up ropes as a form of exercise, but I'd like to find him and congratulate him for ruining my life.

Denton divided the class into three teams. "First team to get all of its members through the course gets a pizza lunch, my treat."

I couldn't win this if my life depended on it. Except now my life kind of *did* depend on it, because throwing non-cafeteria pizza into the mix was like throwing a banana into a room full of starving monkeys.

"Worth playing for?!" Denton shouted, and everyone responded with a symphony of grunts and hoots.

Yours truly ended up on the same team as Todd (yes, *that* Todd) and all his muscle-bound cronies. The only girl on our team, Becky Winstead, had recently placed third in the entire state in gymnastics. I might as well have been wearing a shirt that said THE WEAKEST LINK.

As everyone walked toward the starting line, The Dorf nudged me. "Nice team ya got there. I sure wouldn't want to be you."

"I don't wanna be me, either," I agreed, tucking my tank top into my shorts. I looked out at the course. The gym suddenly seemed enormous. "But at least we'll win."

The Dork smirked. *"They'll* win. You, however, should ride on Todd's back."

"You're about as funny as a submarine with a screen door."

"And *you're* about as funny as walking into an antique shop and asking 'what's new?'" The Dorf patted me on the back.

My teammates grimaced when I moved over to their group.

"Don't screw this up," Todd snarled. "We want pizza." The other behemoths nodded menacingly.

Coach Denton brought the whistle up to his lips. "Hey," I whispered to Todd. "I need that money you owe me, okay?"

Todd narrowed his eyes. "Just worry about winning for once, dorkus."

Denton's whistle blared, and like eager little hamsters,

we dove toward the first obstacle, a dozen low-rising balance beams. I hit the floor and scrambled forward. The beams barely came a foot off the ground, but I was small, and I could soon hear my competition falling behind me.

I burst out from under the beams and kicked my leg up just in time to avoid a hurdle. My toe caught on the second one and I stumbled, but managed to recover over the next few. I might not have been Olympic material, but I wasn't embarrassing myself, either. Todd and his lackeys grunted and snorted behind me, struggling to propel their massive bodies over their hurdles, and only Becky moved fast enough to gain ground for our team.

By now my team was easily in first place. Everything came down to that last obstacle.

The rope climb.

Each team had a designated rope with little flags tied at the top—one flag for each team member. In order to win, everyone had to climb the rope, retrieve a flag, and bring it back down.

Becky went first for our team and retrieved her flag in about half a second. Todd and his overgrown peeps managed to haul their hefty weight up with their tree-trunk arms, and soon only one flag remained.

It was my turn. I looked over at the team with Chucky, Suzie, and J.J. on it. They had just gotten to their rope, which meant I had plenty of time to climb up there and win it all.

I looked up. The top of the rope seemed to be a million miles away. I took a deep breath and remembered what Dad once said about running into a burning building.

When lives are on the line, it's all about doing, not thinking.

"GO!" Todd growled in my ear.

I began to climb. Within a few seconds, the muscles in my arms were on fire, and my sweating palms kept losing their grip. I slipped and slid down a few feet.

Todd and my teammates groaned in disgust, but I grabbed the rope again. I wasn't giving up yet. Our competition already had two of their flags and were catching up, fast. I gritted my teeth and pulled. Halfway to the flag, my muscles screamed again and my palms were on fire. *Is this stupid rope made of barbed wire?* I couldn't go farther, so I clung desperately to the rope and tried to find some strength. I dared a glance down and saw a mash of sneering faces.

My incompetence had allowed The Dorf's team to catch up. And on the other team, only Suzie Walters needed to retrieve her flag. It was down to me against her.

She looked up at me, grabbed her rope and smirked.

It's on, she mouthed. I *had* to get moving.

Grunting and snorting and making noises I didn't even know I could make, I climbed, hand over hand. Suzie was making good time, and in just seconds, we were neck and neck. Her teammates cheered wildly, and, surprisingly, my teammates were cheering *me* on too. I felt a rush of energy.

I weighed a thousand pounds, but the flag was in my sights. It didn't look so far away anymore.

I heard a groan from Suzie. She was struggling! *I might actually win this thing!*

With a final surge, I reached for the flag, fingers shaking from fatigue and adrenaline. But just as I was about to grab it, I made the mistake of looking down again.

I blinked. I couldn't believe it.

The lost kid from the diner was standing behind my team, looking up at me. He wasn't wearing a fishing hat anymore, but it was definitely him. His sandy brown hair was short and choppy, like he'd cut it with a weed whacker. His brows rose in surprise when our eyes met. And then . . .

He vanished into thin air—poof. Adios.

What the—

I was so jolted by the vanishing act that I let go of the rope. I tumbled through the air and braced myself for the unforgiving smack of the gym mats below. *Would I survive a fall from this height?*

I saw Suzie, high above me, grabbing her flag. It was over. And then, suddenly I wasn't falling anymore.

"Nice effort, Stone!" Coach Denton barked. I was *in his arms.* He'd caught me. Then, without warning, he unceremoniously dumped me on the floor, and I smacked the mat like a sack of flour. I didn't know what was more embarrassing: the fact that he'd cradled me like a baby or the fact that Suzie's team was now hugging her while glee-fully chanting "Peetz-a! Peetz-a! Peetz-a!"

"Hit the lockers, everyone!" Denton shouted.

I sighed in defeat, still on the ground as Todd and my teammates stared down at me.

"You're dead, Stone," Todd snarled. "Dead *meat*."

3

142:12:39

"IF YOU WANT YOUR CLOTHES, come and get 'em!" Todd's bellows echoed through the locker room. Next to him, his goons snickered.

I had jammed myself into a locker but could see Todd had my jeans and T-shirt over a toilet. He could have found me in less than two minutes if he wanted—he just enjoyed the game too much to end it.

"Your loss! Have fun wearing your gym clothes all day!" My stuff dropped with a splash, and Todd flushed while the guys gave him fist bumps.

"And I'm *really* not paying you for that oil change now!"

That made my blood boil. I could live with him humiliating me for losing, but Mom and I needed every dime we could get, and I had *earned* that money.

With my heart pounding, I grabbed the locker door.

"What's going on in here?"

Coach Denton entered the room, and I stayed put. Todd sidestepped in front of the toilet to keep Denton from seeing my wet clothes.

"Nothin', Coach," he replied, sweet as can be.

The two-minute warning bell for the next class sounded.

"Then I suggest you get moving," Denton warned. "We need you, Byers. You won't do anybody much good if you're sitting on a bench in next week's game 'cause of too many tardies."

"Right, Coach. Sorry." Todd and his buddies hightailed it outta there.

Denton paused in the doorway and squinted. "Is somebody in here?"

I held my breath, but after a few moments he shrugged and left. I exhaled just as the final warning bell sounded. I only had thirty seconds to get there without being late, so I grabbed the locker door handle and . . . it was stuck.

I yanked harder, but it wouldn't budge. *What if I'm trapped?* I imagined the headline: SON OF HEROIC FIRE-FIGHTER FOUND DEAD OF STARVATION IN GYM LOCKER, CLOTHES STUFFED INTO TOILET.

"No!" I slammed myself against the locker door until it finally popped open, sending me tumbling to the floor in a twisted heap.

"Ouch." I rubbed a new bump on my head.

"Need a hand?" someone said behind me.

I whirled around. That freaky kid was here!

I scrambled backward and jumped to my feet.

"Man, what is your *problem*?" I snapped, my chest heaving.

"Sorry about what happened earlier. I didn't mean to startle you. I just wanted a front row seat for your victory."

"*Victory*? We lost because of me," I shot back, taking an angry step closer. Then I raised an accusatory finger. "Because of *you* and your . . ."

Vanishing act, I wanted to say, but it sounded too crazy, so I lowered my finger and stayed put.

"I do apologize. I had such high hopes for our first meeting, but after yesterday and now today, well . . ." The kid sighed and shrugged. *"C'est la vie."*

I said nothing, so he added, "That's French. Beautiful language."

I sat down on a bench, dumbfounded. "You're seriously nuts. Who are you?"

"I'd rather not say yet. I don't mean to be cryptic, but—"

"Why are you following me? Are you lost? Did you just move here?" I got up again as my voice started rising. "You're in the wrong school!" I cried, throwing up my hands.

"You have questions," he said deliberately. "Entirely understandable."

"Stop talking like that!"

He tilted his head and furrowed his brow. "Like what?"

"Like a grown-up! You sound like you're in a school play or something! And how did you, uh . . ."

I knew I'd have to say it sooner or later.

"—disappear?" I whispered.

"The actual mechanics of it are complicated."

Enough. I turned for the door.

"Something is coming, Benjamin." The kid's voice cut the room like a knife. "Something dangerous."

I stopped. I'm still not sure why.

"It'll be here in just under six days," he added grimly. "A hundred and forty-two hours, to be exact."

"Coming where?" I sighed. "What are you *talking* about?"

"To Earth. It could mean the end of mankind. The end of . . . everything." What little color he had in his face drained away.

I sighed. "Again with the mankind stuff. You should try playing with kids your own age—"

The kid held his hand up. "I'm part of a group. An initiative, if you will, to protect the planet. It's no mistake: We have proof, Benjamin."

I wasn't frightened anymore. Just annoyed.

"First of all, my name is *Ben.* Only my grandmother calls me Benjamin and she's like a hundred years old. Second of all, who's 'we'? What is this 'group'?"

"I'd rather not say until you've agreed to accept." The weirdo was stubborn, that's for sure.

"Accept what?"

"What I *hope* is your destiny," he replied, eyes brightening again.

He was serious. *The end of mankind? Destiny?*

"Nice try, Junior," I stepped forward and reached for him. "C'mon, I'm taking you to the principal's office."

The second I made contact with his hand, he grabbed me and held on. Then something amazing and terrifying happened. I instantly felt my body breaking down, dis-assembling into a billion pieces in the blink of an eye. I felt no pain, only warmth. For that split second, I couldn't see anything, couldn't hear anything. In a purely physical sense, I, Benjamin Thomas Stone, didn't exist.

And then I was back, and it felt like I was being dunked in a tub of ice cubes. My lungs burned with icy air. Most of my body had been reassembled, and my skin, still wear-ing gym clothes, covered me in an instant.

I gasped, dizzy, as I felt the ground under my feet again. The kid clasped my hand tightly as I wobbled. For a lightning-fast moment I saw the final pieces of him being put back together as well.

I shivered and looked around. *We were outside.*

It was night, and so dusty that I couldn't see more than four feet in front of me. It was like a snowstorm of gray, and I was shivering in my gym shorts and tank top.

I screamed and pulled away from the kid. "Where is this? *How* is this?"

He held up a hand. "Relax."

"Relax?! I'm going crazy and you want me to relax?"

"You're not crazy," he assured me.

"What did you do?" I demanded. "Make us . . . teleport

21

or something?" I couldn't believe I was using the word "teleport" in a sentence. But the kid nodded. In fact, he smiled, like he was impressed I'd thought of it.

"How did you do this? Magic?"

He shook his head. "There's no such thing as magic."

The psychotic eight-year-old was now the voice of reason.

He showed me his other hand. There was a little round device, not much larger than a quarter, in his palm.

"*That* little thing?" I spat, squinting for a better look.

"Size isn't everything," he replied matter-of-factly.

"Where are we?"

He held out a hand. "See for yourself."

I was scared, but who was I kidding? I had to look.

I walked forward slowly, the air still too murky to see much of anything. The strange dust stuck to my clothes and hair and eyelashes.

"This way." The kid passed me and pointed to the right.

A pale glow peeked through the haze, and the dust thinned as we moved in that direction.

We emerged and I blinked a few times. What I saw before me was a real-life nightmare.

Devastation.

We were in the middle of a destroyed city. Pieces of some buildings still stood, their jagged edges sticking up from the ground like skeletal fingers.

The light.

I looked up and saw the source of that pale yellow glow.

It was an oval moon, with points at the top and bottom. *Another* one, identical to the first, peeked out from behind it.

With every nerve in my body on overload, I looked down and realized that the crunchiness under my feet was shattered debris from the destruction.

But something else, too.

Bones. *Lots* of bones. And they definitely weren't human.

There was a skull with three eye sockets and a strange, elongated jaw. The wind blew ash from its bared teeth.

I looked to the kid, aghast. I couldn't believe what I was about to say.

"You teleported us to another planet."

He nodded, those strange eyes of his staring intently into mine. "Indeed."

4

"I DIDN'T WANT YOU to have to see this," the kid sighed as we walked through the devastation, "but you left me no choice."

I'd never left Texas, and now I was on *another planet.* Was I dreaming? I tried pinching myself. *Maybe Mom wasn't kidding when she said eating a burrito before bed could cause nightmares.*

We walked down a street littered with strange vehicles, round as fishbowls with a dozen small wheels at the base. Most had been burned, reduced to husks.

"What happened here?" I breathed. The sky overhead was spotted with purple and gray, as if even the planet's atmosphere was covered in bruises.

"They were attacked," the kid said softly.

"Is anything here still . . . alive?" I wondered. Did I *want* anything to still be alive?

The kid shook his head. "We began to detect evidence of the destruction here some time ago—space debris, and sound waves produced by explosions. A faint distress signal. Back then, we didn't have the technology to even *know* that it was a distress signal, much less decipher it."

"Can you decipher it now?"

"Oh, yes. Our technological advances in the last few years have been stellar."

"What did it say?"

I noticed the kid's hands tense. For the first time, he was afraid.

"Dredmore. Whoever or *what*ever did this is called Dredmore. And it will penetrate Earth's atmosphere in six days."

My stomach clenched like it was churning with glue. "You're talking about more aliens?"

The kid nodded, then began walking again.

"How can you know for sure?" I asked, following.

"We've been tracking them from the moment they came into our view parameters last week. Before that, they could have been anything—asteroids, meteors, dead satellites that drifted off course; we just couldn't be sure."

"But now you are?" I pressed. I still couldn't shake the feeling I was in a dream. It was like the afternoon I found out my father died. I came home from school and Mom was already home. I stood there in the doorway for a long moment before going inside. My gut already knew what had happened, but I didn't want to accept it.

"One hundred percent sure," the kid confirmed, his voice thick with the weight of it. "Otherwise you'd be in Biology class right now."

I had so many questions, but I didn't know where to begin. And I was still shivering. Walking in the middle of an ash-covered war zone will do that to a person, especially if that person is wearing gym shorts and a tank top.

"How long have you been stalking me?"

The kid flapped his hands like he was shooing away my words. "*Scouting* you . . . Long enough to know you're the one we need."

A terrifying thought barreled into my head. I stopped walking.

"Is something wrong?" he said.

My heart was practically tripping over itself. This was all starting to make sense.

"You're an alien, aren't you?" Just hearing myself ask that out loud forced me to take a cautious step backward. As I did, something crunched under my foot. The bone was long and looked heavy. If the kid came at me, I would grab it and fight him off.

"I assure you I'm human, Benjamin."

"You sure do like *assuring* me of things, but I wasn't born yesterday," I said. The kid exhaled loudly. "And that teleporting hand buzzer of yours? It's got 'alien' written all over it."

I covered my mouth in case the kid tried to jam an alien

embryo into it. I have this little rule about being impregnated with alien babies: I avoid it.

"This thing?" he asked, opening his palm again. "It's just a machine, built by our techs. Wires, circuitry—"

"What about *that*?" I shot back, pointing at him.

He looked down. "What? My shirt?"

"Very funny. No, *you*. No offense, but you *stink* at being an eight-year-old! Just admit it. You're a lizard or something under that little kid disguise!"

The kid's face twisted into a flabbergasted scowl. "I assure—I mean, I'm *not* a lizard."

I looked into those strange eyes of his. The craziest thing was, I *did* trust him. So I let my guard down. A little bit, anyway.

"I still need answers."

"We have a weapon," he said pointedly. "We think it's potentially the *greatest* weapon humankind has ever had in its possession. And we believe that tapping into this weapon's ... abilities ... is the surest way to protect Earth."

Hmm. Now we're getting somewhere.

"What kind of weapon?"

"I'd rather not say yet, and before you question that, let me explain. I need your mind to be open, without preconceived notions of what you're about to do. It's imperative for this ... project ... to be a success."

"What exactly *am* I about to do?"

The kid took a step toward me. This time I stood my ground.

"Travel to London and begin your training."

Whoa. I definitely didn't see that coming.

"Training for what?"

"To protect Earth from the coming threat."

"What about school? What about my mom?" I felt a little dizzy.

The kid just watched me with a little smile.

"Take a look around." He held out an arm. "This will be Earth if we don't stop what's coming. Your school, your friends, your teachers . . ." He trailed off, but I got the point.

I looked off at the destruction in the distance. These poor beings had probably lived lives very much like ours.

"You're sure I can help stop this from happening?" My voice trembled. The kid, too short to reach my shoulder, patted my elbow.

"I'm sure," he replied softly. If there was a chance I could prevent this from happening to Earth, then I had to take it.

The kid was looking at me with wide, hopeful eyes, waiting for my answer. I took a deep breath. The cold wind felt like daggers, but I didn't mind. I needed the jolt to say what I was about to say.

"Okay. I'm in."

"YES, OF COURSE. I'm so proud of him, thank you," my mother gushed into the phone, "but if you don't mind my asking—why such short notice?"

I stood a few feet away, leaning against our kitchen counter. Mom was in her waitress uniform and had already worked a morning and afternoon shift. Today was her day to work a split, but she'd be home for another hour.

"Oh, you did?" She covered the bottom half of the phone. *"Where's the mail from yesterday?"* she whispered.

I rushed into the foyer to a cluttered table. I grabbed the stack of envelopes, then bolted back and handed it to her. Her eyes widened when she found what she was looking for.

"You know what," she said into the phone, her cheeks

29

turning red, "I'm sorry, it did come. Sometimes it takes me a few days to get around to—"

She stopped talking. I moved closer to get a look. The envelope had a fancy crest on it and said THE ROYAL ACADEMY OF SCIENCE. I could hear the guy talking to Mom on the other end of the line now. He had a deep voice and a British accent.

"I appreciate that, yes," Mom was saying. "I'm sure Ben will be thrilled. Again, thank you. Good day to you, too." Then she hung up.

"What was that about?" I asked.

"Why didn't you tell me about placing first in your school science fair?" she said, hands on her hips.

Uh . . .

"I guess I forgot."

She tore into the envelope. "The man on the phone said it was some kind of *worldwide* science fair. Did your science teacher know that?"

Uh . . .

"He might have mentioned it," I lied. The kid had made me promise at least three times that I would play along. *Billions of lives are at stake,* he had cautioned.

"The winners are being flown to London, all expenses paid, to participate in a weeklong convention. You really knew nothing about this, Ben?" Hands on her hips again. Not a good sign. She was irked.

"Well . . . I knew *something* about it, but I couldn't be sure it was real, so . . . I didn't mention it."

30

Not entirely a lie that time, I convinced myself.

"It's definitely real," she insisted. She pulled out the envelope's contents. "In fact, he said a car is on its way here right now to take you to the airport . . ." She trailed off and stared wide-eyed at the paper in her hands.

"What is it?" I asked, and she handed it to me without a word. I leaned against the kitchen counter again—otherwise I might have passed out right there on the faded yellow linoleum.

It was a check made out to me, Benjamin Stone, for TEN THOUSAND DOLLARS.

"But . . . what . . . how . . . " I stammered. My shock quickly gave way to exhilarating visions of me running into the nearest electronics store and buying the biggest TV they had, then driving it home in a new sports car that would make Todd's precious pickup truck look like it belonged atop a trash heap.

Mom hungrily examined the rest of the envelope.

"It's your prize," she read. "According to this, it's meant to start a college fund for you."

Oh. *Good-bye, mega-TV and sports car, you were nice while you lasted.*

"Who exactly did you talk to just now?" I asked, trying to sound casual.

"Something Pellinore. I wasn't prepared for that accent of his. I figured it was just someone playing a prank at first. His first name was something with a P," Mom said. "Yes. *Peter Pellinore.*"

The name sounded familiar.

"Oh my!" Mom suddenly cried, giving me a jolt. "I have to pack you a bag!" She raced out of the kitchen. A split second later I heard stomping around upstairs.

"I guess that means I can go," I said to the empty kitchen.

I went upstairs to find Mom dashing back and forth between my room and the hallway closet. In her hand she held Dad's old duffel bag from work.

"I've got socks, underwear, extra jeans, a few shirts," Mom rattled off as she whizzed past me. "Just make sure you unpack as soon as you get there so the clothes aren't wrinkled. I don't want you looking like you live in a gutter."

"Sure thing, Mom—"

"Oh, and you'll need a jacket. I think it gets cold in England." She looked up as if pulling thoughts out of the ceiling. "And it rains! Oh no, do you know where the umbrella is?!"

She was seriously losing it.

I rolled my eyes. "They'll probably have umbrellas there, don't you think?"

She stopped to bite at her lower lip, nodded quickly, and said, "Maybe you're right." She whirled away again, disappearing into the bathroom.

I looked to my right and saw that the door to Mom and Dad's bedroom was open. Since Mom usually slept on the couch downstairs now, the master bedroom had become something of a museum. I stepped inside and picked up a framed photo of me, Mom, and Dad. It was taken a couple of years ago on Dad's birthday, when we took him out to dinner at his favorite steakhouse. The three of us had never looked happier. Would we have smiled like that if we had known what the future had in store for us?

Mom stood in the doorway, holding the duffel bag all zipped up and ready to go. "Can I take this picture with me?" I asked softly.

She swallowed a lump in her throat just as a car horn honked outside. As we rushed downstairs, I stuffed the framed picture into the duffel bag.

When we reached the landing, her eyes turned glassy. "Call me every night before bed, and in the morning, too, when you wake up. And maybe also at lunch. Call the diner if I'm not home. You have the number, right?"

"Yes, Mom. I've called it a million times," I groaned. As I hugged her fiercely, I took in the sight of our tiny den. It wasn't much to look at, but there were a ton of memories in that room. *Am I insane to be leaving like this? If the end of mankind is just six days away, am I making a mistake by not spending these final days with Mom?*

Two more quick honks came from outside.

Mom and I turned to the front door. "That Pellinore said the driver would see to it that you got on the plane safely. And he said someone would be waiting for you when you land in London, too," Mom said a little breathlessly.

I nodded, afraid that if I spoke, she would hear how nervous I was. This was really happening. I was about to leave home for the first time in my entire life.

"Maybe I should come to the airport with you—" Mom began, but I shook my head.

"I'll be fine, Mom, I swear."

She gave me an almost helpless look, then grabbed me again for another hug.

"This is all so sudden," she said as she held me tight, her voice shaky.

Tell me about it.

She released me, so I grabbed my duffel and opened the screen door, making my way outside before she could protest. I had already rushed to the limo by the time she stepped outside and onto the porch.

I yanked open the limo's side door, threw my bag onto the back passenger seat, then looked to the front to see the little kid sitting behind the wheel. He was sitting on a stack of books, to be able to see over the dashboard.

"You gotta be kidding me," I hissed.

"Get in." He motioned urgently. *"Fast."*

I jumped into the limo and rolled my window down to wave good-bye to Mom before turning back to him. "Are you sure you can drive?"

"Belt up. Safety first!" he said cheerfully.

As we drove off, I turned and looked through the back window at Mom, still rooted to our porch. And then, as we turned a corner, she was gone.

I suspected that the life I had always known was gone, too, for better or worse.

6

137:46:02

THE SOUNDS of the city exploded in my eardrums.

"Welcome to London," the kid said, letting go of my hand. Teleporting was getting easier to handle, but I still swayed as I fought off the dizziness.

We were standing in the mouth of an alley, looking out onto a grim gray sky and a cramped London street. Cars crawled down two narrow lanes as they passed us; a black cab stopped suddenly for a businessman in a long coat. Behind them, skinny brick houses stood squished together, their tightly packed storefronts advertising everything from souvenirs to fish-and-chips to discounted night tours through haunted London ("For a Jolly Good Fright!"). People were everywhere, talking in British accents. My hand tightened around the handles of Dad's duffel bag. When everyone around you suddenly sounds nothing like you do, it's a little weird.

"Follow me," the kid instructed. "We're already late."

Buildings crowded in on either side of us, the bricks stained and cracked, the ground littered with garbage. There was an angry hiss as I sidestepped a street cat foraging for food.

"Here we are." The kid sighed happily as we arrived at a battered door covered in graffiti.

"*This* is the Royal Academy of Science? Not very royal-looking."

"That was just a ruse for the parents. This is Headquarters." The kid looked left and right (as if anyone else would want to come down this stink-hole alley) and pressed a finger against a nearby brick. A perfect line of small light beams shot out from the doorway, concealing us behind projections of shimmering brick walls.

"A hologram or something?" I croaked. "I thought that kind of stuff was only in movies."

The kid rolled his eyes. Another brick next to the door spun around to reveal an electronic scanner.

"This is a dental scanner," he explained. "An intruder would need all my teeth, in formation no less, to gain access. The walls have been fortified against teleportation, in case anyone managed to get their hands on this." He flashed the device in his palm.

He bent down and put his mouth to the scanner, grinning like someone was taking his picture. A red ray of light panned from right to left, and with a quick *beep-beep* the light turned green. "Hold on," he warned.

I shot him a wary glance. "For wha—"

We suddenly plummeted downward, our feet somehow glued to the square slab under us as we plunged deep below ground. We jolted sideways through a dark tunnel before ascending again—all in less than two seconds—and then we lurched to a stop.

I wobbled, trying hopelessly to catch my balance. I could feel a pull from beneath me, and a tingling throughout my feet and legs that somehow held me in place.

The kid smiled. "The metal is magnetized to bond with the mercury in human blood. Very revolutionary." He gave a satisfied nod.

There was a beep, and suddenly the pull was gone. He and I stepped away, and the slab whisked back down into the darkness. I gulped at the sight before me. We had arrived in the center of a huge, circular room lined with doors. The walls—solid steel, reinforced with millions of bolts all arranged in crisscross "X"s—were maybe fifty feet high, and the floor, made up of marble tiles, was so shiny it looked wet.

On the ground, people carrying clipboards scuttled hurriedly from door to door. Their lab coats all had three letters stitched over the chest pockets: "RTR." From what

I could overhear, most had English accents, and nobody was anywhere *near* my age, but they didn't seem surprised at all to see us here.

I looked up. There were three levels of doors, some twenty and thirty feet up, but with no stairs anywhere. On the *ceiling*, huge red numbers were counting down, like a giant digital timer: 137 hours, 32 minutes, 12 seconds . . . 11 seconds . . . 10 seconds . . .

I nudged the kid. "What is that?"

"The time left until the aliens arrive," he said.

I tensed. A hundred and thirty-seven hours didn't seem like much when it could mean the end of the world. A pretty woman walked by, her hair up in a neat bun. On her way past us, she gave the kid a warm smile. "Good to have you back, sir."

A grown woman, calling an eight-year-old "sir."

He shook her hand. "Fabulous to *be* back," he said brightly. "Where are the trainees?"

"Medical." She gave me a nod as she passed, but I was more interested in her clipboard. At first it looked pretty standard, until I realized the single piece of paper on it was a paper-thin computer screen. And I mean *paper* thin. Two words at the top of the screen sent my pulse racing: PROJECT X-CALIBUR.

The kid led me across the lobby to a spot just in front of the doors. "Stay close," he instructed, and the floor panel we were standing on suddenly *rose up. That's* how the people here got to the second and third levels of doors.

Problem was, I was so caught off guard that I windmilled and dropped my duffel bag. It toppled over the side, landed on another floor panel, and triggered it to *also* rise up. The bag kept rolling, only to hit *another* floor panel—up and down, in a circle, all around the atrium, until it finally came to a rest.

Tell me this isn't happening.

From where I stood at the third-level doors, I could see the workers below startled by the sudden chaos. One poor guy hung on the edge of a rising column, legs flailing, before finally pulling himself up to safety. They all turned to glare up at me.

"Sorry," I winced with an apologetic little wave. I turned to the kid. "Haven't you ever heard of regular elevators?" I hissed.

He shrugged. "Live and learn." He pushed open the door in front of us.

I looked in and saw an Asian kid with spiky hair. He stood shirtless, his legs bent and his arms out as he swayed side to side. *Was he surfing?* But there was no board, or much of anything else, around him except for a few chairs and a couple of white curtain dividers.

I hesitated. This place was a little nuts.

"There are only friends here, Benjamin. No enemies," the kid who brought me here coaxed.

I took a deep breath and stepped into the room.

"See you soon!" Suddenly, the kid was gone, and the door was replaced by wall.

When the Asian kid saw me, he stopped "surfing" and jogged over.

"What up? I'm Kwan!" He looked my age, lean, but not skinny, and really tan. He was about my height, but he was definitely more athletic than me.

"You don't have an accent," I noted.

"I'm Korean American. Emphasis on *American*." He stood tall, chest out.

"No, I mean you don't have an English accent."

"So what's your name?" The words came rapid-fire. This kid had energy to spare.

"Ben. Ben Stone." I held out a hand, and Kwan shook it with both of his.

"Where ya from, Ben Stone?"

"Texas—" I barely answered before Kwan shouted over his shoulder. "Hey, Big Guy, another American! Texas this time!"

Another kid stepped out from behind one of the white curtains. He was also my age, with a puffy baby face and a buzz cut, but he was at least a foot taller than me and Kwan, and big. Not muscular, just bulky, like a hairless bear.

"Tyler's from Florida," Kwan chirped. "Check this out—he wrestles *gators*."

"And crocs. Don't forget the crocs," Tyler said with a calm smile. Even though he was a foot taller than me, his presence was somehow less in-your-face than Kwan's.

"But no croc or gator is a match for you, right?" Kwan slapped Tyler on the back. Hard. He had guts, that's for sure.

Tyler paid him little mind. "The tourists pay to see me win," he shrugged. "I give them what they want."

"What's your deal, anyway?" Kwan asked me.

I was lost. "My deal?"

"Yeah. What do you *do*? Like, I've won more surfing championships than anybody else on the planet under eighteen years old. I've been on the cover of *Sports Illustrated Kids* twice. And you already know what he does." He nodded toward Tyler. "Ten million hits on YouTube!"

Kwan snapped his fingers on both hands and pointed at me. "So what do you do again?"

"Well, I go to school," I fidgeted. "And I work on cars sometimes."

They stared back at me.

"Mostly oil changes. I charge fifteen to twenty dollars, depending on the car." I was kinda proud of that last part.

"So you *race* the cars?" Kwan prodded.

"No. I don't have a driver's license."

"Hmm," Kwan managed. Tyler frowned like someone had just farted.

"Benjamin?" Another door appeared at the other end of the room, and a middle-aged woman in a white lab coat stuck her head in. She looked dignified and well put together, but her eyes were narrowed and her mouth was puckered up like she had tasted something sour. "Are you ready for your physical?" she asked, and I realized that her puckered expression had nothing to do with me; she looked like that all the time.

I nervously glanced at Kwan. He grinned. "Don't sweat it, Earnhardt. We already did it. Piece of cake."

"Earnhardt? I told you—I don't race cars."

Kwan's grin just got bigger. "Whatever."

Sourpuss handed me gray shorts and a matching tank top with RTR printed on the front. "Put these on and meet me inside," she instructed.

After changing behind the white curtains, I left Kwan and Tyler and walked into the next room. It was much larger than the changing area, and everything was steel and glass. In the back corner, another kid my age was running on a treadmill. While he wore the same gray shorts and tank top as me, he was four or five inches taller and looked like a quarterback or something. He had a wide jaw, and his hair was cut short and neat.

Kwan was a champion surfer, Tyler was apparently a Florida tourist attraction and internet sensation, and this kid looked like he would grow up to be a movie hero. What the heck was I doing here?

"Step here, please." Sourpuss pointed me to a round piece of metal on the floor, raised about three inches. I took a deep breath and stood on it.

"Begin physical," she said flatly, and a cylinder of light rose up around me, until I was standing inside a shimmering green tube. Images began blinking along its surface: readings, measurements, scans of my skeleton and veins. Then it all winked out of existence, the light tube gone. A holographic data report appeared in its place, hovering a few feet in front of me. It had my name at the top, along with a bunch of data: height, weight, blood type, and dozens more things that meant nothing to me.

"You can step off now." Sourpuss looked through the report.

"I don't have to . . . run?" I nodded toward the other kid. He was really going at it now like his life depended on it. I spotted his name at the top of the report hovering next to him: MALCOLM GUNN.

"No. Pellinore ordered additional pre-testing on Malcolm." She lowered her voice. "I think he's grooming him for X-Calibur. But you didn't hear it from me."

Excalibur? The sword used by none other than King Arthur?

The door suddenly opened and the kid who'd brought me here stuck his head in. "We need the trainees in the atrium, ASAP. How's he look?" His eyes met mine for a moment.

"His cholesterol and glucose levels are a tad high," Sourpuss said. "He eats too much junk food."

"But not a deal-breaker?" the kid said hopefully.

She nodded disinterestedly. "Not a deal-breaker."

Malcolm had gotten off his treadmill and was walking past us, head high.

"Hey," I said, but he kept going out the door, like he had more important places to be.

"How's *he* look?" the kid whispered.

"Stellar. Head to toe," Sourpuss replied. The kid's shoulders seemed to sag a bit.

Two minutes later, I was in my old clothes, in the middle of the round atrium again. Kwan and Tyler stood to the side of me. Kwan now wore flip-flops, bright red and orange swim trunks, and a shirt that said "Heaven Is a Fifty-Foot Wave." Malcolm was on the other side of me, dressed in a crisp white shirt and cargo pants, along with military-style black boots. He'd been running like a maniac just minutes ago, but he looked completely unfazed.

Another trainee—a girl—was also here, standing a few feet away from the rest of us. She was a couple of inches shorter than me, and stocky, built like a fire hydrant. Her hair was all one length, to her shoulders, and hastily pushed back behind her ears. Her skin was pale like most everyone else here, and she was wearing gray leggings, sneakers, and a faded yellow shirt with a peeling Pac-Man logo. She saw me looking at her, so I smiled, but she crinkled her nose and looked straight forward again.

"Darla Dill," Kwan whispered. "From Seattle. One of the best video game players in the world."

"Really?" I turned to him. "How do you know?"

"Tyler and I met her already. Plus, she was on the cover of *Video Game Monthly* last month. And *eleven months* in a row before that."

Wow. I really had to start reading more.

"But her last name totally suits her," Kwan added. "She has the personality of a pickle."

Across the atrium, a single door opened. The lab workers had gathered behind us, and my mysterious eight-year-old friend joined the group. There was a second or two where nothing happened, and then . . . a man appeared. He was a tall, middle-aged guy wearing a dark, pin-striped suit that looked like it cost more than my mom made in a year. He had thick black hair, slightly wavy, and he was clean-shaven, with a strong jaw and eyes that narrowed with purpose. More than anything, though, I was struck by the way he carried himself. Everything about him oozed confidence as he walked toward us. There was little doubt he was in charge here.

"Good afternoon. And welcome to our Round Table Reboot," he boomed in an English accent.

Round Table Reboot. RTR. Project X-Calibur. Things were starting to make sense.

"Everyone ready to get started?"

"Affirmative," Malcolm instantly replied in a solemn English accent.

"Somebody needs to cut down on the caffeine," Kwan whispered to me with a chuckle.

"Do you ever shut up?" Darla hissed under her breath at Kwan.

"My name is Pellinore," the man said. "Percival Pellinore." It took a moment for the name to register, but then it hit me: Percival Pellinore was one of the original knights of the Round Table, *a guy who had fought alongside King Arthur.*

Pellinore held out a hand to the adults all around us. "And this is my team. Techs, scientists, engineers, physicists. The cream of the crop in their fields, all chosen to work under the utmost secrecy. I owe them a great deal. And very soon, so shall mankind."

Pellinore walked over and put his hand on the shoulder of the eight-year-old. "And this, of course, is my noble and esteemed partner. He has been by my side—and I by *his*—longer than I care to remember sometimes."

The kid smiled. These two had history. He gave us a little bow. "Greetings, new knights. My name . . . is Merlin."

THE MERLIN? The greatest wizard of all time? I *had* to be dreaming!

I stole a quick look at Merlin's eyes. No wonder they had looked weird to me when I first met him: They were the only part of him that still showed his true age.

"Have the five of you had a chance to get acquainted?" he asked.

"Well, Ben and I go way back," Kwan wisecracked. "And Tyler here—the croc killer—is like my brother from another mother—"

"I would never kill a croc," Tyler interrupted. "We wrestle. There's a difference."

Merlin and Pellinore exchanged a look. Darla said nothing, her expression tight.

Malcolm looked at me, hesitated, then came over and

warmly held out a hand. "I've met everyone except Ben here. Pleased to meet you. I'm Malcolm."

He had a really strong grip. "How did you know my name?" I asked.

"Saw it on your data sheet earlier. During your physical."

"Oh. I saw yours too, actually. Cool name. *Gunn.*"

He gave me a curt smile. I was pretty sure he was only being friendly because Merlin and Pellinore were watching.

I decided to follow Malcolm's example. I turned to Darla, extending a hand myself. "*We* haven't met yet, either. I'm Ben."

She reluctantly shook. "Darla," she said simply, avoiding my eyes and basically introducing herself to the floor.

"All right then," Pellinore continued. "You'll have plenty of time to get to know each other later, knights."

Knights?

Pellinore nodded to one of his techs, and the guy walked over with a thick stack of folders. He put his hand on them. "Can any of you deduce the contents of these files?"

"Battle plans, sir?" Malcolm ventured.

"Admirable guess, but no, Malcolm," Pellinore said appreciatively.

"Restaurant take-out menus?" Kwan offered with a smirk.

I traded a glance with Tyler. He took a step backward, as if trying to blend into the background (hard to do when you're the biggest kid in the room).

Pellinore grabbed a handful of the folders and held them up.

"These are other candidates we scouted for this project. Dozens and dozens around the world who might have had what the RTR needs." He suddenly tossed the folders over his shoulder, and they fluttered to the floor. I don't think anyone expected that. I certainly didn't.

"We've chosen *you* five," Pellinore announced, striding toward us. "Do not take this honor lightly." He glanced at Kwan. "That said, we're going to give you an opportunity to leave now, if you wish."

Huh? Leave? Merlin was watching me now, surely wondering if I'd leap at the chance.

"What's ahead for you is nothing short of a monumental undertaking. 'Dangerous' doesn't begin to describe what's headed toward us." He eyed each one of us gravely. "And if we fail, it will be the end of everything we hold most dear."

I swallowed, remembering the destruction I had seen with Merlin.

"Look at the faces around you, knights. When battle comes to us in"—he glanced up at the digital countdown— "one hundred and thirty-five hours, some of them might not make it out alive. Any one of *you* might not make it out alive."

There was silence as the stakes sank in.

"Well, *I'm* not going anywhere." Malcolm crossed his arms and gave us a fixed, determined look.

Pellinore grinned. He homed in on me, Kwan, Tyler, and Darla. "Any one of you might also be *replaced*—today, in fact—if you don't have what it takes to succeed here. We cannot afford to waste precious time on anyone who isn't ready to give his or her all. Mankind deserves more than that, don't you agree?"

Kwan, Tyler, and Darla nodded. I crossed my arms, fighting off a chill. The atrium was cold, or maybe it was just the shiny steel all around us that made it seem that way, like standing inside an enormous, well-lit freezer. There was a part of me—a big part—that wanted to go home and tell Mom we needed to protect ourselves from what was coming. But then I thought about Dad. How many times had he chosen to rush into a burning house or building? What would *he* think of me turning my back on a chance to step up for mankind?

"I'm staying," I said softly, probably more to myself than anyone else. Malcolm glanced over at me, and Merlin too.

"Why us?" Darla suddenly asked. I'd been wondering that too.

"Because you each have qualities we believe will be beneficial to our task."

"But we're *kids*," she pressed.

Pellinore exchanged a glance with Merlin. "That information is on a need-to-know basis," he explained. "And right now, you don't need to know. But soon. You have my word."

He held a hand forward. "Now, if you'll follow me,

we've got some more initial testing to get out of the way. Then you'll be shown to your rooms."

Two double doors slid open to reveal a hallway with orange lights glowing down the middle. It looked like the tunnel of a secret military base. As we walked past Pellinore and Merlin, I whispered to Kwan, "My father told me all the King Arthur stories. When Merlin was born hundreds of years ago, he was an old man already, with incredible wisdom and power. He ages *backward*, really slow. That's why he looks like a kid now—"

A hand suddenly rested on my shoulder. I stiffened. It was Pellinore.

"It's Ben, right?"

"Yes, sir," I gulped.

Pellinore kept pace with me as we continued through the corridor. "I couldn't help but overhear that you're well-versed in Arthurian legend. Where are you from?"

"Texas."

"Any brothers or sisters?"

"No, sir." I felt like I was being interrogated.

"Forgive me for the questions. It's just that I know so little about you. I've had a very involved hand in choosing the others here, but Merlin alone has championed you, and quite enthusiastically, at that."

Championed me. I stared straight ahead as we continued walking, unable to meet his gaze.

"What do your parents do?"

"My mom is a waitress. My father . . . is dead."

It had been a while since I had had to say that out loud. I think Pellinore noticed, because his eyes softened. Then he turned to everyone.

"There are no secrets within these walls," he said, holding out his arms. "The creatures living in the shadows of our universe are very real. *Magic*, however, and some of the other things you may have heard in the legends surrounding Merlin and I, are not." He stood taller than ever, as if to prove that he was still worthy of our respect.

"But Merlin's a wizard," I blurted. How could there be no such thing as magic when the greatest wizard of all time was standing three feet away from me?

"The knights of the Round Table were feared and respected in their day, as was I," Merlin explained as we all continued walking. "But much of our prowess began with creating our own legends. Arthur was particularly creative in that regard—"

"The best," Pellinore said to himself fondly.

"Don't misunderstand us, knights," Pelinore added. "Not all of the legends are total myths. We *did* fight hard and often, against many worthy foes. We won many battles, went on many real quests. Arthur and I tracked down the Holy Grail, and the holy water I drank from that cup resulted in my very real immortality. But our greatest weapon was the fear our opponents carried before we ever set foot onto a battlefield."

Merlin stopped and looked me in the eye. "We'll need more than bloated myths to defeat what's coming. We may not have genuine magic, but think about it, Benjamin—the magic of today is our technology. And *that* will be our weapon."

I glanced at the other kids. They were entranced, although Malcolm had a cold look in his eyes. I don't think he enjoyed Merlin speaking directly to me.

"Okay," I offered softly, even though the closest I'd come to modern technology in my life was my desktop computer at home, an ancient piece of junk that Dad bought for me secondhand. I glanced past Merlin and noticed a door up ahead. Wherever we'd been headed, we'd arrived.

Pellinore straightened his suit jacket and held a hand forward. "Now that we've settled that, let's proceed. There's much to do, knights. *Much* to do."

8

134:28:11

I FOUND MYSELF strapped into a strange metal chair that looked like something you'd find at a dentist's office on Mars. The other four knights were seated in identical ones, all of us lined up in a row.

Sourpuss was here, overseeing a group of techs as they checked our restraints, while Merlin and Pellinore stayed behind her, watching silently. The room was far taller than it was wide, shaped like an elevator shaft. Even though the metal of the chair itself was cold against my skin, the air in here was warmer than in the atrium; I could feel a light sheen of perspiration on my forehead.

"These are two necessary stress tests," Sourpuss explained, all business. "We're looking for medical anomalies that we might have missed earlier."

"What's that mean? Medical anomalies?" I fidgeted,

trying to get comfortable. The chair was in serious need of some cushions.

"Overactive photo- or audiosensitivity, undetected bone or joint weaknesses that might hamper your ability to handle g-force duress," Sourpuss counted off on her fingers. "Not to mention possible mental instability brought on by—"

"This is all just precautionary, knights," Pellinore interrupted gently.

"I'm sure it'll be fine, Ben. No need to be afraid," Malcolm said, looking over at me. He was at the end of the line to my right, one chair past Tyler. I *was* afraid, but why did he have to say it in front of everyone? Kwan, Tyler, and Darla looked at me like I was going to run home to Mommy.

"All good," I mumbled, avoiding their gazes.

Sourpuss continued. "You'll notice that there's a button under each of your hands. Your directive is simple. When you hear a tone"—she held up a finger and a low beep sounded throughout the room—"press the button corresponding to the ear in which you heard the tone. Is that clear?"

I looked back and forth between Tyler and Darla on either side of me. Tyler looked confused and whispered nervously to me, "I just heard it in both ears. What do I do?"

Suddenly, I felt a slight vibration and looked up to see a pair of mechanical goggles unfold out of the back of the chair. Darla looked really nervous, although I would never call her out on it like Malcolm had done with me.

Once the goggles settled over my eyes, they pushed my head back into the chair. There was a tiny suction sound as the eyepieces fastened to my face, leaving me in pitch black. Ear buds were jammed into me. It was like being blind and having someone suddenly stick a cold finger into each ear. I did all I could to keep from panicking— *breathe in, breathe out.*

"Can I get a large popcorn with extra butter?" Kwan joked from behind his goggles.

There was a muffled, aggravated sigh from Sourpuss. "Let's begin. And if you close your eyes, I'll know. *No cheating,*" she warned.

I blinked a few times and tried to steady myself, even though I had no idea what was about to happen. "Good luck, everybody," I said, but the only response I got was a sudden beep in my left ear. I quickly pressed the corresponding button.

A second beep came right after that one, then another one, now in the right ear. As the beeps continued, I felt myself settling in; this wasn't so hard after all. But then I spotted a small white dot of light ahead of me, to the lower right. The goggles were starting to *do* something.

The light pulsed and then suddenly streaked right at me, leaving a light trail behind it like a comet. I instinctively dodged to the side as if trying to avoid it, but then another one, this time red, came from the other direction. Dozens of light streaks blazed across my vision like a multicolored strobe light. What about the other knights?

Darla had definitely looked nervous about those goggles. And what about Kwan and Tyler and Malcolm? Were they okay? The thought of having to witness *any* of us having a bad reaction to this test frightened me. The assault was getting overwhelming: It felt like my head might explode, but I had to focus and keep pushing the buttons.

And then . . . it was over. The ear buds retracted from my ears and the goggles lifted off my face with a *wha-slurp* sound, giving up their hold on my skin. It was like having an octopus yanked off my face. I looked over at the others. Thankfully, nobody was shaking uncontrollably or foaming at the mouth, though Darla's shoulders were slumped. Malcolm actually had a big, ridiculous grin on his face.

"You all passed," Sourpuss called out. "A couple of you—Benjamin and Darla—by the skin of your teeth."

I was surprised to hear my name, until I remembered that toward the end of the test I had been worrying about everyone else, and I'd forgotten to push my button a few times. I saw Merlin's smile falter at the news and clenched my jaw. I exhaled, eager to be freed from the chair. But they weren't done with us yet.

"That was the easy part," Pellinore announced. "On to phase two."

9

133:46:26

FULL DISCLOSURE: I'll never again hear the word "g-force" without practically wetting my shorts.

After the first test, the chairs—including the floor panels below them—suddenly rose up higher and higher, until the five of us were forty feet above the floor. Sourpuss's voice came through speakers in the corners of the ceiling. "Your directive for this second part of the test couldn't be simpler: *Hold on.*"

I gulped. I wasn't overly afraid of heights, but I was afraid of *falling*.

"You going to be okay this time, Earnhardt?" Kwan asked.

"I was fine on the first part, Kwan," I shot back. "I just—"

I didn't get to finish, because we all reclined backward until the five of us were parallel with the ceiling. I knew from science class that heat rises, and that was certainly the case now. Forget an elevator shaft, the room now felt like a warm chimney. The ceiling was just a few feet away from us. It was a network of pipes, giving off more heat.

"I've got a bad feeling about this," Tyler murmured.

"Yeah, it's called the *end of the world*," Kwan quipped.

WHOOOSHHH!!! It felt like my stomach and everything else inside me was going to come out of my mouth. My cheeks and lips and hair felt like they were being pulled upward as the rest of me, fastened to the chair, plummeted. I squeezed my eyes shut, waiting to smash into the floor and be turned into oatmeal.

We came to an immediate stop just a foot above the floor, all five of us still in reclined positions. Our chairs rose up on their columns again. Within seconds, we were again staring at the ceiling.

"I went on a ride like this at a state fair once," Tyler groaned to nobody in particular. "I barfed afterward. Fried cucumbers and corn on the cob. Not pretty."

That image made my stomach lurch, and just as Kwan yelled "Yee-ha!!" we all dropped again. I waited desperately to hear Sourpuss's voice—hopefully saying, *They all passed; help the kids out of those torture devices ASAP.*

"Good, now let's flip them around," she said instead.

I did *not* like the sound of that.

This time, when we got to the top, the chairs continued to recline backward and *kept going*, slowly turning all the way upside down until we were facing the floor, forty feet below. I had thought this couldn't get worse. Wrong: Not being able to see the ground was *way* better than this.

We dropped again, and the ground came rushing at us at lightning speed. I was overcome by a crushing fear that we'd plunge through the floor, deeper and deeper into HQ, never to be seen again. We stopped a foot from the floor again, my heart thrashing against the strap around my chest.

"That should do it," Pellinore called. "Get them out." The techs helped us out of our chairs. I tried to walk with confidence, but I felt like I had just taken a ride inside a washing machine on the spin cycle.

"How do we feel?" Pellinore asked exuberantly.

We? I'm sure *he* felt fine. I, however, practically had my intestines stuck between my teeth.

"Never better," Malcolm grunted, standing tall and looking good as new. The dude was seriously getting on my nerves. Sourpuss scanned me, Tyler, Kwan, and Darla with her eagle eyes. "Any soreness or pain I should know about? Withstanding g-forces of this magnitude will be essential to your success. Speak up now or suffer the consequences later."

The four of us gave each other quick glances. Kwan and Malcolm were all smiles, Tyler and Darla looked a ghostly shade of white, and I was crossing my arms, trying to hide my sweat-soaked armpits.

None of us said a word.

• • •

Later in the bathrooms, I stood at the sink and splashed cold water in my face. I had some lingering nausea, and I was exhausted. Malcolm stood next to me at another faucet, washing his hands. He stole a quick glance at me in the mirror.

"Rough start, eh?" he asked casually. I nodded.

Kwan came up behind us after flushing in a stall. "They probably hit us with the tough stuff right away to see if we could handle it, that's all. From here on out, I bet it's smooth sailing."

Tyler joined us. "Defending the world against *aliens* is going to be 'smooth sailing'?" he asked dubiously. For once, Kwan didn't have a wisecrack.

"Did Merlin already tell you what we're going to be doing? How exactly we're going to fight them?" Kwan asked me eagerly, then leaned over the sink to wash his hands.

"He must have told *you*, right?" Tyler pressed. "You're his *champion*."

I grabbed paper towels and dried my face. "No. I don't know any more than you do, I swear." In the mirror, I noticed Kwan and Tyler exchange a look, like they were considering whether or not I was lying. I didn't like it. And Malcolm was just watching me again, leaning up against the bathroom wall. *Examining* me.

"Whatever." Malcolm shrugged it off. "We should get back outside."

A few minutes later, we all gathered in the atrium again.

"From this point forward, knights, think of headquarters as your Camelot," Pellinore boomed. "We're a *team*, with a duty like no other in the history of time. And speaking of time—"

He snapped his fingers and five techs approached, each holding a shiny metal contraption with a hole about five inches across. "Your arms, please," said Pellinore, pointing to the holes.

Malcolm stepped forward and fearlessly stuck his arm into the box nearest to him. I saw Merlin watching me, so I also stepped up. I slid my arm into the metal tube. There was a sound like a high-powered hydraulic pump and a *clack* of two metal pieces coming together, and then I felt something warm around my wrist.

"All done," the tech said, so I pulled my arm out. I had a strange-looking wristwatch installed on my arm. The band was solid metal, with no clasp, and had been melded together to fit me perfectly. The digital watch face was large, but simple. No buttons, no extraneous readouts like the temperature or date. In fact, it wasn't even giving me the *time*. It was a countdown watch, to match the clock on the atrium ceiling.

"We have a problem, sir," one of the techs said to Pellinore. "I'm terribly sorry, but we seem to have miscalibrated one of the devices."

It was Tyler. His thick forearm had gotten *stuck* inside his watch installer. With five techs yanking on the box at the same time, Tyler's arm finally came out with a loud pop. But his countdown watch was in place and unscathed.

"It's imperative that everyone's first priority here is the task at hand," Pellinore explained. "The countdown until the aliens' arrival should be foremost in all our thoughts."

I looked around and realized that all the techs were wearing countdown watches too, mostly covered by their lab coats. Pellinore and Merlin were the only two people not wearing one.

"Merlin, would you care to escort the knights to their rooms for the night, or shall I?"

Merlin nodded. "I'll take them."

"Wait," Malcolm interrupted. I tensed. *Now what?*

"I hope I'm not out of line for asking, sirs, but is there a gym I can use for an hour or so? I'm not ready to sleep yet."

"Not out of line at all, my dear boy!" Pellinore replied happily. "I had planned to show you the exercise facilities in the morning, but no time like the present! Come, knights! What we've got is far better than any gym you've ever seen!"

10

132:26:08

AT FIRST, the gym looked like an empty room, with a shiny black tile floor and padded white walls. But if there was one lesson I had learned in my short time at HQ, it was this: Never take anything at face value.

Pellinore walked into the room and held out his arms. "Maintaining prime physical condition is vital to the success of any warrior," he said. Out of the corner of my eye, I noticed Tyler discreetly suck in his gut. "Strength, agility, endurance—all essential for each of you. But time is of the essence, and we are *knights*! We have our own methods of preparing for battle!"

I looked around at the padded walls in confusion. Was he going to make us fight each other?

Pellinore walked over to a wall and opened a hidden panel. My eyes widened. There were *swords* lined up in a rack. The thought of swordfighting in the same room with *the* Percival Pellinore, an original knight of the Round Table, was beyond exciting.

Pellinore took off his suit jacket, revealing muscles clearly visible beneath his shirt and tie. For a dude who was hundreds of years old, he was in awesome shape. As he pulled a sword from the rack, the blade began to pulse blue in three places—near the tip, in the middle, and at the base. It wasn't a regular metal sword: It was constructed out of a heavy-duty plastic of some sort, with sensors built into the blade.

Pellinore, sword in hand, walked over to stand in front of the opposite wall. He flashed us a grin, then announced to the wall, "Prepare to fight!"

The five of us looked at each other. Was he going to attack *us* now?

A panel in the wall slid up, revealing a sight that made us all gasp—even Malcolm's jaw dropped.

A robot stood inside the nook, holding a sword of its own.

"I . . . am . . . Iron Man," Kwan growled in amazement and stiffly moved his arms up and down like a robot. I couldn't help but grin.

The robot stepped out and waited silently. It was six feet tall, with arms and legs made of steel rods that had glowing blue sensors everywhere. The droid's face was flat, with nothing except two blue glowing eyes and a blank expression. But there was still something unsettling about its stare.

"Knights, this is a spar-bot," Pellinore explained. "A mechanized sparring partner used to stay in shape. Not only is he able to fight, but he can score the performance of his opponent by recording his or her moves with his eyes." Pellinore circled around the spar-bot, pointing to different sensors as he moved. "In addition, he tallies the hits he receives, so keeping track of your progress as a warrior is effortless."

Pellinore loosened his tie, then faced the spar-bot and lifted his sword, assuming a fighting stance. *"En garde!"* he shouted, and the spar-bot sprang to life. I hadn't been prepared for how well it *would* move—just like a person, and fast. Kwan's stiff robot impression had been *way* off.

"Pay attention, knights!" Pellinore shouted as he sprang into action. "This is called a *lunge!*" He jabbed the tip of his sword into one of the spar-bot's torso sensors. There was a beep, and the sensors flashed from yellow to orange to red, depending on the power and accuracy of the blow. Pellinore whirled impressively and bounced a few steps back.

That's what a real knight looks like, I thought.

"This is a retreat! And then . . . a *fleche!*" he shouted as he flung himself at the spar-bot again, arm outstretched, scoring another hit, then continuing *past* it. The spar-bot struggled to find its target. Even though the mechanical fighter moved fast, Pellinore was faster.

"And now a *beat*," he barked. Sweat flew from his brow as he struck his blade against the spar-bot's blade, over and over.

The spar-bot took a wild lunge at him, but Pellinore blocked the attack with his sword and shouted to us, "A parry!" He pushed the spar-bot back with a heavy grunt, muscles flexing. The steel fighter toppled backward and hit the ground. Pellinore wasted no time. He jumped onto the spar-bot, one knee on its chest, and held the tip of his sword to a sensor at the spar-bot's throat. There was a long *BEEEEP* and the spar-bot's eyes and all of its sensors flashed bright red before going dark and lifeless.

Pellinore turned to wink at us, entirely in command. "And I win."

We clapped wildly.

"I'm next!" Malcolm called.

"Then I'm after Malcolm!" Kwan followed, but Pellinore held up a hand.

"Relax, knights. There's no need to take turns." *Four more* wall panels slid up to reveal four more spar-bots.

"Whoa," Tyler gaped. "Iron Man has brothers."

The new spar-bots were identical to the one Pellinore had just fought. They stepped forward in perfect sync and then froze—a tiny spar-bot army. Malcolm lit up and turned toward the rack of swords, but Pellinore held out an arm and looked across the room, where a couple of techs had entered.

"Are the knights' sparring uniforms completed yet?" Pellinore asked the techs, but they shook their heads.

"Your instructions were that the knights wouldn't need spar gear before morning, sir," one explained anxiously.

Pellinore nodded. "Very well." He turned back to us. "It'll have to wait until tomorrow, Malcolm, although I admire your enthusiasm."

"Can't I just spar in my regular clothes?" Malcolm countered.

Pellinore shook his head. "The risk of injury is too great." He put a hand on Malcolm's shoulder. "We need you. Don't forget that."

Malcolm beamed, and I now understood why the others had been so interested in my connection with Merlin. Even though our cause was greater than any one of us, I couldn't help but feel jealous of Pellinore's apparent fondness for Malcolm. Most of my life had played out like that stupid obstacle course in gym class: I'd give my all, taste the possibility of winning and being special, and then fail in a blaze of glory, once again proving that I wasn't cut out to be anything except average. I did not want that to happen again.

I glanced at Merlin. He was watching me, his expression hard to read. If I was ever going to be a hero, it was now or never.

11

130:11:48

"THIRTY-FIVE, THIRTY-SIX, thirty-seven," Malcolm grunted, doing push-ups next to his bed. Just watching him made me tired.

Darla got her own room, but Kwan, Tyler, Malcolm, and I were sharing. The room was easily large enough for the four of us, with a window that looked out on London spanning the entire far wall. Even though some of HQ was below ground, the part that contained our rooms was apparently several well-concealed stories above it. Outside, the hazy gray air made the city look like something from a Jack the Ripper horror movie.

Malcolm and I had two beds on one side of the room; Kwan and Tyler had beds on the other. Each had a futuristic steel nightstand, and above the headboards, two large flat-screen TVs had been fixed to the walls. Right now they were showing only that maddening countdown (as if the ones *permanently installed on our wrists* weren't enough).

"Hey Kwan—what are you doing?" I asked, noticing him alone in the corner, ear pressed to the wall.

"Shhh. Trying to hear what Darla's up to in her room."

"Why?"

He shrugged. "She's weird, that's all."

Tyler kept pushing buttons on his phone, but his sigh told me he wasn't getting anywhere. "I just wish I could tell 'em about this end-of-the-world stuff," he moaned. "I have a little sister. What if they can go someplace to hide, or—"

Malcolm stopped doing push-ups, either because he had reached a hundred or because Tyler had annoyed him. Probably both.

"We'd *all* like to tell our families about this," he said, wiping a bead of sweat from his brow. "But unless you were told something different than I was, we have to keep it a secret for now."

"Why?" Tyler pressed, his brow creased with worry. Kwan had stopped listening to the wall and flopped on his bed.

Malcolm shook his head and shrugged. "Pellinore has his reasons, that's why."

"But what if we fail?" Tyler continued. "I don't want my family to die because they didn't even *know* they were in danger."

After a moment of heavy silence, Malcolm stood up and stretched. "We're not *going* to fail. I don't know about you three, but I intend to kick serious alien butt." He turned and headed toward the bathroom. "I'm taking a shower."

After he was gone and we heard the water running, Kwan whispered, "What crawled up *his* butt?"

"He's definitely intense," I muttered, then tilted my neck from side to side, trying to get rid of a cramp. "Man, that g-force test turned my spine into spaghetti."

"You don't think there's going to be any *real* tests here, do you?" Tyler grimaced. "Like in school. Questions and answers?"

"Obviously we're going to be in fighter jets or something," Kwan theorized. "Or maybe inside missiles that'll get fired at the aliens. Why else would we have to take a g-force test? Only pilots do that kind of stuff."

He had a point. "But what good would it do to have us inside missiles? Wouldn't we just die when they exploded?" I made a little "poof" with my hands.

He deflated a bit. "Yeah. That would be bad. Unless . . . they need us inside the missiles to turn 'em on in the air?" His eyes grew wide as he sat bolt upright. "That would explain why they need kids! 'Cause we're small! No wonder Mr. P. said it was a need-to-know basis. If we knew we were going to die, we'd all get the heck outta here!" He snapped his fingers, convinced.

Tyler gulped. "Do I *have* to blow up inside a missile?"

71

I rolled my eyes. "We're not going to be inside missiles. Besides, if they had kids here just because of size, why would Tyler be here?" I held a hand out in front of Tyler as if I was showcasing a new car on a game show. "He's *not* small."

Tyler's face brightened as if I had just saved him from certain death. "You're right!"

Kwan threw up his hands. "Whatever."

We heard the shower water stop. Kwan glanced over his shoulder. "I bet hotshot in there knows something. Pellinore seems to really dig him," he whispered.

I considered telling them what I had heard about Pellinore "grooming" Malcolm for X-Calibur, but decided against it. I didn't want them to think I was privy to any more information than they were.

"But Merlin picked *Ben*," Tyler countered. "Isn't that just as important?"

I wasn't in the mood to get on the discussion of Merlin championing me again. "What we do know is that this whole project is called *X-Calibur*, right?" I said quickly.

"So?" Kwan asked.

"So, the legend of King Arthur and the knights of the Round Table was all about a super-powerful *sword* called Excalibur," I explained, leaning closer like I was telling a story around a campfire. "At first, nobody could even use the sword because it was stuck inside a big stone. A bunch of people tried to pull it out, but nobody could." I paused

72

for dramatic effect, just like Dad used to do with me. "Until . . . Arthur came along."

Tyler leaned closer. "Then what happened?"

"Arthur became king after that. And *leader* of the—"

I stopped when I spotted Malcolm standing in the bathroom doorway. He had changed into shorts and a T-shirt for bed, his wet hair combed back. For a moment I was struck by how much he looked like a young Pellinore.

"Leader of the what?" he asked.

". . . the knights." And that's when I spotted something on the wall under the window: a small control panel with buttons. I crossed the room.

"Any idea what this is?" I wondered, running a finger over the panel.

"Try pushing one of the buttons," Kwan prodded, joining me.

"No way—" I began, but a hand reached between us and pushed one with no hesitation. It was Malcolm.

"No risk, no reward," he said coolly, looking at me. *Challenging* me. I probably would have said something in return (something equally cool, I'm sure), but I was too busy gaping at the window. Instead of looking out at foggy London, we were now looking out at a dazzling beach. The sky was a vivid blue, and so was the ocean. In the distance, a group of dolphins was diving in and out of the water. The whisper of an ocean breeze and the relaxing *shu-sshhhh* of waves.

"Whoa," Tyler gawked. "Is that real?"

"I don't think so." I pressed another button that had a little "up" arrow on it, and the view changed again. This time it was a desert, the pristine sand stretching for miles.

"It looks so real," Kwan gaped. "You sure the entire HQ didn't just teleport somewhere?"

"Of course not," Malcolm snapped, then hit another button, bringing us back to the original view of London.

"*This* is the only real view. The others are probably just a relaxation technique. I bet you're going to need it, too."

"How can you be sure the London view is real?" I challenged. "Maybe they're *all* fake."

He sighed and jabbed a thumb at the glass. "I walk those streets every day, remember?"

Oh. Yeah.

"Well, at least we have something to look at now," Kwan grumbled, then jumped onto his bed again so he could reach one of the large countdown clocks. "If you ask me, Mr. P. is cuckoo about these countdown clocks. I'm surprised he didn't have them installed on the insides of our eyelids, so we'd see them in our sleep."

"I'm sure he considered it," I muttered.

Malcolm got into bed. "Lights out," he announced.

Kwan reeled as if punched. "No offense, bro—but who made you camp counselor?"

"You heard what Pellinore said. Tomorrow's going to be busy. It's either lights out in here or I'm going to ask for my own room. I intend to be at my best tomorrow."

The three of us exchanged a look. He had a point. Five minutes later, we were all in our beds. Even with the curtains closed and the lights off, the two large countdown clocks bathed us in an unsettling red glow. My brain swirled with a million different thoughts. The next few days were going to be tough enough without being under a microscope because of my connection to Merlin. *Why* had Merlin chosen me, anyway? Why would *any* kids be chosen to defend the world?

I looked to my nightstand, where I had placed the framed photo I brought from home. Me, Mom, and Dad. Smiling. Like it was another lifetime. I turned my focus to the countdown clock on the opposite wall instead, watching the seconds as they ticked down. Forty-two seconds. Forty-one seconds . . . forty seconds . . .

When sleep finally came, I dreamed that I was standing in the atrium of HQ. But it was eerily deserted.

"Hello?" I called out, but the only answer was my voice echoing back to me a dozen times. Two doors slid open, startling me, revealing the hallway we had been in earlier. The ceiling lights were dark, the hallway shrouded in shadow.

As I walked to the mouth of the hall, the light nearest me suddenly started pulsing, beckoning me. I took a cautious step, and another light above me lit up, as if *guiding* me somewhere. I swallowed and looked back over my shoulder.

Just like that, I was suddenly outside, back in Texas,

watching Denny's diner from the parking lot. It was a gorgeous day—clear sky, gentle breeze—and the diner was bursting at the seams, probably a Saturday afternoon. I could see guys from school in there—laughing, smiling, eating burgers and ice cream. Todd Byers, The Dorf, everyone.

And Mom, too. She was in her waitress uniform, bustling from table to table. My eyes widened when I saw her give a slice of apple pie to . . . Dad. He was seated with a bunch of the guys from the firehouse, all of them in their bulky gear and covered in soot. Mom and Dad glanced at the window and saw me. They gave a little wave, but just as I lifted my hand to wave back, the sky over the diner opened up in a flash of blinding white light. I shielded my eyes.

Then the diner exploded in a mass of flames and debris.

I woke up with a jolt, my chest heaving. I looked to the countdown clock on the wall, then the one on my wrist. I had only been asleep for *two minutes*.

I gulped; it was going to be a long night.

12

121:02:57

I AWOKE TO THE SOUND of someone knocking.

"Who is it?" Malcolm called out from the floor. I looked over the side of my bed. He was already awake, back to his push-ups. I groaned. *You've gotta be kidding me.*

"I've got uniforms for you, knights. And breakfast," came a voice from the hall.

Malcolm got to the door first (shocker, I know) and whipped it open to reveal a bespectacled, disheveled young tech. He had a large metal cart with four sets of clothing boxes sitting on top. Malcolm immediately grabbed a stack. I spotted my name on another one and did the same.

"There are pajamas and everyday wear, padded sparring outfits if you choose to work out in the gym, and flight training jumpsuits," the tech explained. "All custom fitted to your exam measurements."

So we *were* going to be flying something—but what?

77

I prayed that Kwan wasn't right about us being stuffed into missiles.

Malcolm had finished changing into his training gear before the rest of us had even opened our boxes. The jumpsuit was impressive—gray with a silver shimmer, as if there was steel woven into the fabric, with a patch on the upper left: the bold letters "RTR" embossed in the middle of a solid black X.

Malcolm stood even taller in his new uniform. He turned to his nightstand and grabbed something from his top drawer. I couldn't see exactly what was clasped in his hand, but it looked like a tattered ribbon.

"When are we going to fly?" Malcolm asked the young tech as he rushed back to the doorway.

"I'm . . . not entirely sure," the tech stammered. "My orders were to bring you the uniforms and breakfast, that's all."

He opened two steel doors on the side of the cart. We were immediately hit by the smells of warm breakfast. My stomach went into a growling fit.

"Normally everyone eats breakfast in the cafeteria, but the schedule today will be too tight for that—" the tech began.

"The schedule you apparently know nothing about," Malcolm cut him off.

"Dude, chill," I murmured to Malcolm, and he turned to look at me.

"When the whole world is watching in five days, *you* can 'chill,' all right?" he snapped.

I kept quiet after that. The ribbon he'd grabbed from his

nightstand had wound him up, big time. He was gripping it so tightly his knuckles were white.

"What've you got in there?" Tyler asked the tech, pushing between the rest of us to get at the food inside the cart.

The tech brightened. On the matter of breakfast options, he had all the answers: "Pancakes and sausage, fruits, pastries, egg dishes with ham, cheese—"

"I'm a vegetarian. Nothing with meat, please," Tyler interrupted.

"*Vegetarian?*" Kwan scoffed. "But you wrestle alligators and crocodiles."

"I wrestle them, I don't eat them," Tyler replied matter-of-factly. "There's a difference."

As the tech handed Tyler a heaping plate of pancakes, fresh fruit, and a piping hot bowl of oatmeal, I looked to my left and noticed Darla standing outside her room, watching us. Her clothing boxes were stacked at her feet, and she was eating an omelet with hash browns.

"Morning," I said as I smiled to her. "Are the eggs good?"

She hesitated a moment, then mumbled "fine" and stepped back into her room. Small talk obviously wasn't her forte. *I guess that's what happens when you become good enough at video games to be a world champion,* I thought.

I turned to the tech. "One of everything you got, please. I'm starving."

With our bellies full (me, Kwan, and Tyler had devoured enough to feed a family of sixteen, but Malcolm only had an apple, a banana, and skim milk), our official tour of headquarters began in a seemingly unending hallway. Even more intimidating than its length, the curved ceiling and walls seemed to gradually slope downward, leading deep below ground.

On my right, Darla's face looked pale as she stared down the length of the tunnel.

"You okay?" I whispered.

"Worry about *yourself*," she snapped. She resumed staring down the tunnel like it was the entrance to a haunted house.

Next to me, Kwan gave me a nudge. "See? The chick has issues."

"Prepare for movement, knights," Merlin announced. He and Pellinore were standing at the front of the group.

Movement? I braced myself, thinking we were about to drop through the floor again, but instead my feet almost slipped out from under me as the floor began to glide forward, like a giant conveyor belt.

"Sidewalk surfing," Kwan grinned. "If only it moved faster."

Pellinore raised an eyebrow and barked an order into the air. "Initiate passenger bond and accelerate, please."

I felt a familiar magnetic pull in my feet and legs, and the floor suddenly *raced* forward with us fixed to it, soaring down the endless tunnel at sixty miles per hour as our hair blew everywhere. We approached the end of the main tunnel in about ten seconds, then made one dramatic turn after another. I cursed myself for eating so much earlier.

"Yee-ha!" Kwan shouted. Tyler had his eyes closed, and I think I actually heard him humming softly to himself, like he was trying to meditate. Darla didn't look pale anymore. She looked *green*. And Malcolm was taking the ride in stride, ribbon still clutched in his hand, a little smile on his face as the wind blew past him.

"Decelerate," Pellinore ordered, and the moving floor slowly came to a stop. After a beep, we were no longer magnetized to the floor.

"*That* was one seriously sick ride," Kwan gushed.

Tyler grimaced and touched his belly. "Yeah. Sick."

We had stopped at an observation window that looked in on a massive room full of techs—dozens of men and women of various ages, all seated in front of holographic touch-screen monitors. Most of the displays focused on satellite images of muddy shapes and sinister-looking specks in outer space.

"This is where our techs monitor the aliens' movements—speed, trajectories, anything and everything that's pertinent," Pellinore explained.

I decided to finally ask a question that had been on my mind for a while now. "Do you and Merlin work for the government? Is that what all this is?"

"Quite the opposite, Ben. The last thing we want is for the governments or armed forces of the world to get involved in this project. In fact, the less people know about us, or the coming threat, the better."

"Why, sir?" Malcolm asked.

But instead of answering him, Pellinore looked up and said, "Next bay, please."

There were no techs in this next room, just one large, ominous black box, a perfect ten-foot-square cube made of shiny black panels. Millions of little lights were blinking over every square inch of it.

"Wow," I breathed. I had no idea what I was looking at, but it sure was impressive.

"You're looking at decades of work here, knights," Pellinore said proudly, and he pressed a button on the wall. After the bay window slid up, we could hear something coming from inside the strange black box. Incredibly, it sounded like a miniature *war* was going on inside. There were the sounds of explosions and buildings crumbling, along with screeching cars and screams.

"What the heck?" Tyler murmured as the lights all over the box began to blink faster and faster.

Just as the cacophony reached its peak, the box suddenly stopped shaking. You could hear a pin drop, and I felt an overwhelming sense of dread; the sudden silence was the non-sound of everything *gone*. And then—

Ding.

A slip of paper appeared, sticking out of a slot in the box's side. Pellinore took a deep breath and grabbed it quickly. He had a look, then handed it to Merlin with a grim shake of his head.

"What's going on?" I asked. "What is this thing?"

"An alien invasion simulator," Pellinore informed us. "Day after day, week after week, it runs war scenarios, analyzing what would happen to mankind if Earth was attacked. Specifically, the millions of possible outcomes that might occur once Earth's governments and armed forces get involved."

Merlin was still looking at the slip of paper when he added, "The outcome for mankind is always the same."

He held up the slip of paper. It had just one word on it: EXTINCT.

13

119:00:49

"INFORMING THE WORLD of the coming threat will almost certainly bring about our extinction." Merlin crumpled the slip of paper.

"But how can you keep *everyone* from seeing aliens when they arrive?" I asked doubtfully. "Won't that be impossible?"

"Next bay, please," Pellinore ordered, and the hallway floor started moving again. I was thrilled to get away from the eerie black box. That thing was the largest, scariest fortune cookie ever created.

The next room was the most impressive so far. It was circular, like the atrium, but at least three times as large, and every inch of space of the curved walls was lined with *thousands* of flat-screen TVs showing broadcasts from all over the world. From a series of control panels in the room's center, lab techs with high-tech earphones closely monitored the footage.

My heart skipped a beat when I noticed a screen showing the early morning newscast we watched at home every day. These techs really were monitoring *every single* newscast, even from Breakwater.

"As you've probably figured out already, this is where we keep an eye on the news," Pellinore said dryly.

"Why?" Kwan asked, but Malcolm was the one to answer quickly.

"To intercept alien sightings. Right, sir?"

"Correct. We must be ready to intercept any and all human communications related to aliens. As you saw just moments ago, we've proven time and again that the aliens' arrival must be kept secret."

"Wait, so even after the aliens show up for battle, nobody will know we're the ones defending Earth?" Malcolm asked, deflated.

"Exactly. This project will always be a secret. Before, during, and—hopefully—afterward," Pellinore replied.

"This is only our first line of defense, knights," Merlin added. His face looked shadowy against the light from the screens behind him. "Once we become aware of intel, we can hijack or block any transmission known to man before it spreads. TV signals, radio, cell phones, internet, email. If people use it to communicate, then we have access to it."

Something dawned on me. "At home yesterday I saw on the news that NASA was tracking space debris headed toward Earth. Are they actually tracking the aliens?"

"Unfortunately, yes," Merlin replied. "But NASA doesn't *know* they're tracking alien ships yet. They really do believe it's just space debris—"

"You mentioned an elite team of fighters . . . You mean us?" Darla asked from the back of the group.

"Absolutely," Pellinore confirmed.

Tyler raised his hand. "Will we be fighting alongside older people, too? You know, adults?"

"Just you five," Pellinore said bluntly.

"You can't be serious," I blurted. I had seen the devastation these aliens were capable of. This was suicide. "How the heck can five *kids* fight off an alien attack?"

Pellinore grinned. "That's where X-Calibur comes in." He looked up. "Accelerate, please. Destination: X-Bay."

The hallway floor *surged* forward, the force so powerful that a few of us swayed backward. I gritted my teeth. The incline of the moving floor got steeper, and we rocketed deeper and deeper below ground.

When the floor came to a drastic stop, I let out a shaky breath. How much more of this craziness could I take?

The curves of the tunnel ended at two enormous steel doors in front of us.

"What do you keep in there?" Tyler asked, mouth agape. "Godzilla?"

"Maybe you can wrestle it," Kwan joked.

An electronic scanner glowed red at the side of the door. Pellinore leaned down and smiled, letting the device get a read on his teeth. The glow turned green and the massive doors slid open, revealing an empty room the size of two football fields, at least, with a ceiling that was a hundred feet high.

With a twinkle in his eye, Pellinore turned and shouted into the vast space. "Reveal X-Calibur!"

Nothing happened. The five of us looked at each other, confused. Had Pellinore and Merlin gone senile in their old age? There was a hiss in the center of the room, along with the faint whirr of gears turning below the floor. A section of the ground suddenly *split in two.*

My hands clenched and unclenched at my sides. As I took a step forward, my mind raced back to the stories Dad would tell me about the most famous sword ever crafted, and how it had been kept in an underground cavern before rising up from a magical lake to reveal itself to King Arthur.

I looked to my left and realized that Malcolm had also taken a step forward, standing next to me, tense with excitement. As the floor opened wide, something rose up on a steel platform.

My jaw dropped. X-Calibur wasn't a sword at all. It was the most kick-butt *spaceship* I had ever seen.

14

IT BECAME CLEAR TO ME that HQ and everything in it had been designed to imitate the look of X-Calibur. The ship was twenty feet long and shaped like a rounded arrow. Its wider front end consisted of four panels with seams that came together to form an X. From there the windowless sides sloped closer together as they got to the tail of the ship, ending in a crisp metallic point. X-Calibur was *beyond* impressive. It was downright . . . *otherworldly*, like nothing that could have ever been created by human hands.

"This is an alien ship, isn't it?" I breathed.

Merlin nodded. "Precisely."

The ship had two short wings that curled at the ends into gleaming points, like razor-sharp steel talons. Were those "wings" there to help the ship fly? Maybe. But they were lined with holes, and inside those holes were tiny globes that held swirling energy inside them—yellow or purple or red, depending on the angle you looked at them, like they had been filled with colored lightning. Even though Merlin and Pellinore had insisted that there was no such thing as magic, the energy inside those round mechanisms seemed like the next closest thing.

"I'm so ready for this," Malcolm whispered.

"Can I touch it?" Darla asked Pellinore.

"Of course, Darla. If we stick to schedule, in roughly forty-eight hours you'll have to do a great deal more than just touch it." He added to the rest of us, "All of you will."

As Darla carefully placed a hand against the side of X-Calibur, her eyes widened. "It's humming!"

Now that she'd broken the ice, the rest of us followed suit. Darla was right: The metal (if that's what it was) felt slightly warm to the touch, and the longer I held my hand against it, the deeper the warmth got. I had the strange sensation that the feeling was moving up my arm. I looked to the others, but they made no mention of it. When the warmth continued up the length of my arm and entered my chest (*was* I imagining it?), I yanked my hand away, startled.

Merlin, who had been watching me all along, smiled brightly. "It doesn't bite, Benjamin."

I managed a nod and walked to the ship's tail. Tyler, Kwan, and Darla followed. There were eight glowing panels at X-Calibur's rear, four on each side, where the body came together to make a perfectly sharp point. The panels were sunken inside recessed cavities, giving off a dim, otherworldly glow. It reminded me of the red-hot embers of a campfire after the flames had died down. I was pretty sure we were looking at the ship's thrusters, or power source.

"Where did you get this?" Kwan asked Pellinore. "I'm guessing they don't sell these at Walmart."

"I found it in my travels, centuries ago."

"Carbon dating on the surrounding rock told us the spacecraft had been untouched for ages. Long before Earth was populated by man," Merlin said.

"What was it doing there?" I asked.

"It was piloted by an extraterrestrial being, I believe. There was a data recorder on the ship. An onboard diary, if you will."

"Where's the alien now?" I looked around with new dread. I wasn't in the mood to be surprised by the appearance of any intergalactic monsters just yet.

"He was long deceased when we found him," Merlin explained. "It took our team many decades to work up a rough translation of his audio diary, but he apparently flew the ship here, to Earth, to hide it from his own people."

"Why would he do that?" Tyler wondered, still gazing at the ship.

"He created this spacecraft as the ultimate weapon," Merlin replied, his voice heavy with respect. "His people had become increasingly violent. A planetwide civil war broke out, and he had second thoughts about letting his creation be used for battle. So he brought it here, to a planet that was still uninhabited at the time. He *sacrificed* himself to protect his own race from his finest work."

Merlin placed a hand against the ship and looked up at it, his ancient eyes filled with hope. "I believe we can make him proud by using his work for good. To protect *our* humble planet."

"Why is it named X-Calibur?" I asked, as Malcolm snooped around the front and sides.

"*I* named it," said Pellinore, then walked to the front of the ship and pointed out the X created by the ship's seams. "In homage to my glory days with the Round Table. Arthur had his sword, and we have a weapon for modern times."

I felt the hairs on the back of my neck stand up.

"Shall we have a look inside?" Pellinore pressed a hand against the side of the ship. A small, previously invisible panel glowed, and a hatch slid up.

"Brilliant!" Malcolm rushed over.

Pellinore patted him on the back. "It took my team nineteen *years* to figure out how to open it."

A set of glowing, holographic stairs appeared from thin air. They didn't look like they could bear even the lightest of us, but Malcolm charged forward, and we heard the unmistakable *thunk* of his boots as he hit each step.

"Whoa," Tyler gasped. "He's standing on light!"

"How's that even possible?" Kwan asked, bending down for a closer look and rapping his fist against the shimmering stairs.

Pellinore sighed. "I wish we knew. We've been trying to figure it out for decades. The aesthetic of X-Calibur, and some of its more . . . *accessible* technology, has steered us in the development of things here at HQ. But much of the rest is, well, still a mystery."

Malcolm rushed into the ship. When the rest of us hesitated, Pellinore urged, "No time like the present, knights. We *are* on a bit of a deadline."

The inside of X-Calibur was as smooth and spare as its outer body. I'd been expecting all sorts of crazy alien buttons and gauges, but there was none of that. And with all seven of us inside, the ship felt a little cramped. It definitely hadn't been designed for this many people: There was only one seat.

And Malcolm was already sitting in it.

"Look at this," he boasted. "The pilot seat fits me like a glove."

Kwan, Tyler, and I moved for a closer look. Malcolm had a seat belt across his waist and chest, constructed out of blue holographic light; two straps projected from the ceiling and crisscrossed his chest to make another X.

There was a control console in front of the pilot seat, rectangular, about three feet long, with a horizontal handle sticking out of each end with buttons on it. They looked like ultra-modern joysticks. I figured that Darla, being our own video game master, would be super pumped about those controls. But when I turned to see the look on her face, she was still lingering well behind all of us again, hanging out by the ship's door.

She's not going to last here, I thought.

"The seat molds itself to whoever sits in it," Merlin explained, and I turned my attention back to the group. I took a better look at the steering console, which bore no markings whatsoever—just a round glass panel, about ten inches across, throbbing as it changed colors.

On the floor beneath the steering console were four more glowing panels, two on each side. I assumed those panels were for the pilot's feet, but I couldn't see any labels.

"Let's have each of you get a feel for the seat," Merlin instructed. "Go on, Benjamin. You next."

Malcolm grudgingly stood up. The seat belt disappeared, and the buttons on the steering console went dark. When I took his place, the console buttons began to glow again, then the holographic seat belt appeared out of nowhere to strap me in. The seat felt like a large hand that adjusted to grip me tighter. It was incredibly comfortable, too. I had to give props to the dead alien dude: He knew how to design a chair.

I reached out to grab the steering handlebars on the console, and the second I made contact, the entire column slid closer to me, moving on a hidden track in the floor. There was a surge of power throughout the ship as the console and floor panels lit up. The curved, blank wall in front of me suddenly became a crystal-clear piece of glass, as if the metallic look of the wall had been simply *turned off* to become X-Calibur's windshield.

Startled, I pulled my hands off the steering console and everything went dull again. The windshield winked off, becoming just the front wall again. I looked to Merlin and Pellinore and the other kids, heart pounding.

"It does *that* for everyone, too," Pellinore said dryly. He motioned for me to get out of the seat.

"So, are we all going to be in here when the aliens show up?" Kwan wondered.

Pellinore shook his head. "*One* of you will be chosen to fly X-Calibur."

"But if the seat molds to fit whoever sits in it, why a kid?" I asked. "Why not find the greatest pilot in the world to do it?"

Pellinore and Merlin exchanged an unsure glance. We all saw it, so Kwan scoffed, "More of that *need-to-know* BS, right?"

I had to smirk. There was something to be said for not beating around the bush.

Pellinore nodded to Merlin, who took a deep breath. "In truth, we would have loved to employ the best pilot we could find. It would have made our job . . . far easier. But we've found that the ship responds best to children."

"*Only* to children," Pellinore corrected.

"How come?" Tyler asked.

"My techs tell me it's most likely a system that requires

a distinct bio-signature range. And that range seems to be a bio makeup under fifteen years old."

"So are we really just five guinea pigs?" Tyler asked. "You wanna see which one of us is best for this thing, and then the rest of us are sent home?"

"Aww, man." Kwan threw up his hands. "I'm missing two surf competitions to be here for nothing."

The mood inside the alien ship was turning increasingly sour. Merlin coughed loudly. "The rest of you will be utilized to the fullest, believe me."

"Doing what?" Kwan snapped. "Twiddling our thumbs in front of a computer monitor?"

Pellinore turned toward to the ship's door. "This way, knights. I'll show you."

We followed him and Merlin across the underground hangar, our footsteps echoing throughout the vast space.

"There will be no thumb-twiddling," Pellinore said. He pressed a panel on the wall to reveal three more spaceships in a second underground hangar. But while Pellinore and his team of engineers had obviously tried to duplicate the alien ship, these new ships were still pale imitations at best. You could see the metal seams all over them, and the windshield was plain glass, always visible. The power source panels on the back looked a lot like regular engines.

"As you can see," Pellinore continued, "we've built four fully functional X-Calibur prototypes that the rest of you will use in battle. My techs have copied everything to the best of our abilities, and I've spared no expense. These ships shall *also* have child pilots. For better or worse, I fully trust the intentions of X-Calibur's creator."

His eyes rested on me, Kwan, Tyler, and Darla as he spoke, further proof that he expected Malcolm to be the one flying the real X-Calibur.

"But, wait—there are only three ships there and four of us," Darla pointed out.

Pellinore turned for a look, confused.

"She's right," Merlin said, his little brow furrowed. "Where is the final ship?"

VROOO-WHISSHHHH!! Another X-Calibur prototype suddenly soared over our heads, startling everyone as it flew around the very top of the hangar airspace.

"What on Earth?" Pellinore practically choked as the prototype roared deeper into the hangar that housed X-Calibur, executing some dazzling twists and twirls along the way.

Someone else was showing off some major skills down here. "Whoa. That dude can *fly*," I gasped.

Pellinore raced over to a panel on the wall and shouted into it, "We've got a one-nineteen in X-Bay! Repeat! One-nineteen in X-Bay! I want full lockdown!"

I whirled to Merlin, pulse pounding. "What's a one-nineteen?!"

Merlin's face was pinched with full-fledged fear: "Intruder."

The alarm system blared throughout the hangar as the

prototype made a sudden flawlessly executed turn and soared past us again before coming in for a quick landing near the hangar entrance. A hatch on the side popped open and the pilot jumped out, stumbling for a moment before finding his footing and running toward the door. He was wearing a gray pilot helmet and matching flight training jumpsuit, just like the ones we were all wearing. But his was clearly not custom-fitted like ours; it hung on him, much too large.

There was no way to see the intruder's face. *What if it's an alien in there?* He was definitely the *size* of a little green man from Mars.

It seemed like the guy would make it to the door, but Malcolm suddenly charged after him. He caught up with the mystery pilot and tackled the dude with a grunt, then flipped him over and held down his arms. I have to admit, it was darn impressive.

Merlin, Pellinore, and the rest of us rushed over as a dozen or more techs in lab coats barreled into the room. Pellinore gave Malcolm a pat on the back. "Good work, my boy!"

I scolded myself. Why hadn't *I* gone after the intruder like that?

As Merlin bent down to yank off the intruder's helmet, I inhaled sharply: We were about to see an honest-to-goodness alien, some horrific creature from outer space here to destroy us all.

Wrong. It was a girl. A very *human* girl. And even with

her hair all messed up from being inside the helmet, she was the prettiest girl I'd ever seen. She had big green eyes, light brown hair with a hint of blond highlights throughout, and flawless skin. No offense to the girls at my school, but nobody looked like her in Breakwater.

"Ivy?" Malcolm gasped, then jumped off her and took several steps backward.

"Hey, Malcolm," the girl said in a British accent. Then she grinned and added, "Nice tackle."

It was kind of cool to see Malcolm so out of whack for once. He and this girl obviously knew each other, but why did he seem so . . . embarrassed? I noticed the stunned look on Pellinore's face. He gaped openly, trying to find words as his cheeks turned red.

"How . . . did . . . you . . . get in here?" he finally seethed. "And how did you learn to *fly* like that?"

Ivy got up and dusted herself off, then gave us all a self-satisfied smile. She was enjoying every second of this. "I can do lots of things, Father. You'd know that if you gave me a chance."

AFTER THE FIASCO WITH IVY, the five of us had been whisked back to our rooms, probably so Pellinore could sort things out with his daughter and avoid any more embarrassment. Although, if you'd asked me, Ivy's introduction to the rest of us was full-on rock star material. Not only had she found a way to sneak into HQ without her father knowing (no easy task), she had seemed to *enjoy* it. The upside of this sudden change in schedule was that we were given a chance to call home.

"What's the royal academy like?" Mom asked. "Is it nice?"

I scooted back on my bed so I could sit against the wall, the phone to my ear.

"The HQ—I mean, the *academy*—is cool. We're, uh, learning a lot already about science and . . . stuff."

My improv skills were starting to crumble. Merlin and

the techs were probably listening in on our calls right now, ready to cut the line if we said anything we weren't supposed to.

I glanced across the room at Kwan. "Yeah, Dad. I *know* it's my last year," he was whispering into his phone. He sounded frustrated—nothing like the happy-go-lucky jokester I'd come to know and (kind of) like. "Just make sure you sign me up for the competition next month. Please."

Next to Kwan, Tyler was also on the phone. When he saw me looking, he turned away uncomfortably, trying to keep his conversation private. I did manage to hear him whisper something about "lots of smart kids here, Ma" and "I'll try my best."

"Sorry, Mom, but they're telling us we gotta get back to work," I sighed into my phone.

"Of course, honey. I love you, and I'm so proud of you," she gushed, making me feel guilty for lying.

"Love you too," I whispered, not wanting to sound too cheesy in front of the others. I felt my gut tighten as I looked up at the big countdown clock on the wall: a hundred and sixteen hours left.

I hung up and turned back to Malcolm's bed, intending to ask him about that medal he was polishing. It was attached to the tattered ribbon I'd noticed earlier; it was what had gotten him so wound up. But now he was standing at his open closet, pulling out his padded sparring outfit. "What are you doing?" I asked.

"Going to the gym," he said flatly. "Do you really think Pellinore would rather have me sitting around doing nothing?" He turned and headed toward the bathroom.

"Wait—how do you know Ivy?" I called out. "When you tackled her earlier, you already knew her name."

That stopped him. "I was just trying to help. You don't think Pellinore is angry about it, do you?" His expression softened with genuine worry. I probably could have messed with his head, but I wasn't going to lie to him, even if he had been kind of a jerk so far.

"Nah." I grinned. "I think he was impressed."

He surrendered a rare smile. "Ivy and I go to the same academy."

"Academy for what?"

"*School*. Same as yours at home, I'm sure."

I was pretty sure Ivy's and Malcolm's "academy" was *nothing* like my school at home, unless of course it had an ancient air-conditioning system that broke down every summer.

"You think Ivy'll be flying with us now?" Tyler joined in now that he'd finished his call home. "She can already rock and roll up there."

Malcolm's smile fell away. "You better hope not."

"Why not?" Kwan asked, also joining us.

"Because unless there's another ship somewhere, there were *five* ships—X-Calibur, plus the four others built by Pellinore's team."

Tyler squinted, not grasping what that meant.

"If Ivy is given a ship, then one of you is out," Malcolm clarified.

"What about you?" I asked Malcolm. "You could be out too, you know."

He gave me a look like I had just said pigs could play baseball. He had zero reason to be worried.

"Not likely, Benjamin," he replied and leaned toward me to make it count.

I stiffened. He'd love nothing more than to see me lose my place here.

"I guess we'll see," I said stoically.

"Guess we will," he replied, stone-faced, and disappeared into the bathroom.

I let out a long exhale. Keeping cool in the midst of Malcolm's aggressiveness could be exhausting.

Tyler whispered to me, "Maybe we should go to the gym too?"

"Are you going to listen to *Malcolm* over Pellinore and Merlin?" I scoffed, already shaking my head.

"I guess not."

Kwan moved to the enormous window screen and flipped through each background, pretending to channel surf. "Repeat . . . Seen it . . . Blah . . . Whatever."

I looked up at one of the wall clocks. Even though it only showed the countdown at the moment, it was still basically a flat-screen TV. *Hmm.* I climbed onto my bed for a closer look.

"You're wasting your time, bro. There are no buttons," Kwan said.

"No remote, either," Tyler added. "I looked everywhere."

There was an inch of space between the TV and the wall, so I grabbed the corner of the TV and pulled. It didn't budge at first, but then it squeaked loose a few inches, revealing an adjustable viewing arm installed behind it. "Anybody have a screwdriver?" I asked.

"Oh, sure. I always travel with tools," Kwan cracked.

"Maybe a dime will work," I suggested, so Tyler fished out a dime from his stuff. I went to work, using the dime to loosen the TV's screws.

"Mind telling us what the heck you're doing?" Kwan barked.

"HQ has been here for decades, right?" I gritted my teeth as I struggled with the screws. "Long before the RTR knew exactly when the aliens would show up. The countdown was probably only started recently. Which means—"

"These TVs were probably *real* TVs before that," Kwan finished excitedly.

"Yup. Remember all those newscasts we saw on the tour? This place is getting a whole bunch of channels already." I pulled the final screw loose and gently pulled at the TV frame. "We just have to find a way to access them."

I had taken apart more than a few old televisions in my day (not to mention rusty toasters, broken washing machines, radios, and just about anything else I could find to play around with), so I felt pretty comfortable giving this a shot. I separated the back corner and looked inside. The good thing about newer TVs is how little there actually is inside them. All of the working guts are contained on one circuit board. The *bad* part is, unless you know what you're doing, that circuit board might as well be a fifty-sided Rubik's Cube. But then I saw something that gave me hope.

"Anybody know what SkyTV is?" I asked. A three-inch cylinder had that name printed on the side of it, with an audio/video feed snaking out of the side. Could it really be that easy?

"SkyTV is a satellite TV provider here in London."

I turned. It was Malcolm, standing in the bathroom doorway in his heavily padded sparring outfit.

"What are you *doing* up there?" he hissed.

"Even if you could get that thing to show something other than the countdown—which I *doubt*—we'd still have no way to change the channel, remember?" Kwan pestered me.

He was right, of course. But a casual glance toward the atmosphere window gave me an idea. I pulled the descrambler through the back of the TV, then carefully yanked on the wire it was connected to. There were at least seven or eight feet of extra wire coiled into the wall. I jumped down from the bed and kneeled next to the window's control pad, using the dime again to loosen its screws. Malcolm, Kwan, and Tyler watched me with baffled looks on their faces.

"Earnhardt's crazy," Kwan chirped. "I *love* it."

In less than a minute I had connected the SkyTV

descrambler to the window's control pad. I gave everyone a wide-eyed grin. "Here goes nothing."

The view of London suddenly disappeared, and the entire window was now full of . . . static.

"Impressive," Malcolm deadpanned. "What do you do for an encore?"

I held up a finger. "Wait for it." Then I pressed the little "up" button on the window pad.

"Holy guacamole!" Kwan gasped as the window displayed a soccer game. The game's announcer yelled "GOOOAALLLLL!" as one of the teams on the field celebrated.

"Let me try that!" Kwan wedged in next to me and hit the "up" arrow again. The channel changed to a cooking show. Kwan grabbed my shoulders and shook me like a rag doll. "You just became my new best friend, Earnhardt!" he shouted.

Tyler also gave me vigorous pats on the back (almost slapping my lungs through the front of my chest). "Awesome, Ben! No wonder Merlin picked you! You're like . . . a genius!"

Malcolm's expression turned so icy that I might have needed earmuffs.

"I wouldn't exactly say *genius*," I mumbled. This wasn't much different from the million times I had taken the guts out of a broken toaster and replaced them with new ones—but I wasn't going to tell them that.

"It's not like we're going to have time for TV, anyway,"

Malcolm said stiffly. "While you bozos watch television, I intend to defeat a spar-bot or two—"

KNOCK-KNOCK. Someone was at the door.

Kwan, Tyler, and I froze in terror. Malcolm turned to give me a grin. "Good luck explaining this one, genius."

"Who is it?" I called out to the door.

"Merlin," the voice replied. *Crap.*

"Just a minute!" Kwan shouted. "We're, uh—"

"We're naked!" Tyler blurted in a panic, catching dumbfounded looks from me and Kwan. Even Malcolm scrunched his nose.

"Sorry," Tyler whispered sheepishly. "It's all I could think of."

I lunged to the window's control panel, disconnected the descrambler, then jumped onto my bed to push the countdown clock back into place, my heart practically exploding out of my chest.

"All good. Let him in!" I whispered, then jumped off the bed as Kwan opened the door. It was Merlin, all right. And Darla was with him.

"Everything okay in here?" Merlin asked. I was pretty sure my knees were shaking. I'd risked everything just so I could impress Tyler and Kwan and Malcolm with a dumb TV? *Stupid, stupid, stupid!*

"Why wouldn't it be?" Kwan asked.

"Yeah. We were just watching the uh, countdown clocks," Tyler added, and he might have been the worst liar on the planet. "But we weren't naked."

Merlin and Darla stood there, lost. Darla frowned.

"Why are you dressed for sparring?" Merlin asked Malcolm.

"I was just about to leave for the gym."

Merlin shook his head. "You're all to come with me right away, dressed in your standard flight training suits. You'll be attending a training session with Nigel Barrington."

"*The* Nigel Barrington?" Malcolm asked, eyebrows raised.

"The one and only."

I had no clue who Nigel Barrington was, and, judging by the confused expressions of Tyler and Kwan, neither did they.

"Will Pellinore be there too?" I asked Merlin. I kind of really just wanted to know if *Ivy* was going to be there.

"Percival will catch up later. Now come—you've all got a great deal to learn." He glanced at me, and I gulped. I couldn't make any more mistakes, or take any more stupid risks.

16

AFTER DOWNING protein shakes provided by the staff, we were sitting at desks that had touch-screens for tops, which were tilted slightly for maximum efficiency. At the head of the spacious room, Nigel Barrington, retired military legend, showed us photos of death and destruction from the alien planet I had *already seen firsthand*. The pictures hovered behind him, ten feet tall, casting an eerie glow around his bulky silhouette. Tyler and Darla gasped as the next grisly image came up. Judging from the pale faces of the other knights in the room, I'd been the only "lucky" one to take a nightmarish trip to the devastated planet.

"Not pretty, is it?" Barrington growled in a gruff British accent.

He was a stout guy in his fifties with a gleaming shaved head. He had a bushy mustache and tree-trunk arms covered in faded tattoos. Though short, he wore a tight black T-shirt, camouflage pants, and *massive* combat boots that made him look like a distorted action figure. The dude was even chewing on a *nail,* which made the dainty cup of hot tea at his side look hilarious.

"Next photo," Barrington commanded. I glanced at Kwan. He was slack-jawed at the jarring images, but he still kept whispering to Tyler animatedly, even giggling at one point, and I couldn't concentrate over his voice.

"This isn't a *joke,* Kwan," I snapped. Everyone turned to look at me. "What if that was our friends or family in those photos? Or any one of us here? Would you joke about that, too?"

Kwan withered. He looked like he wanted the desk to swallow him whole. I didn't want to embarrass him, but I couldn't help it. The memory of what I'd seen on that planet still hurt.

"It's okay to be scared," I told him quietly. "You don't have to hide behind jokes all the time."

At the front of the room, Barrington nodded. "If you're not scared—any of you—then you're not *human*. The greatest warriors throughout time have had fear—difference is, they make it work for them." Then he took a sip of tea.

"Sorry," Kwan mumbled. He refused to look in my direction. I had a pretty good idea I was going to pay for this one way or another.

Barrington walked closer, standing among our desks. He smelled like leather and tea spices. "Now, we've studied the victims of Dredmore extensively and concluded that the race of aliens on this devastated planet was, for lack of a better term, *weak*."

Dredmore. The word felt like a dark wind passing through the room.

"Know yourself and you can win the battle," he preached. "Know your enemy—"

"And you can win *the war*," Malcolm finished for him.

A devilish grin made its way onto Barrington's face. "Right you are, my boy. Our enemy's aim is to *kill*." He stomped his enormous boot and snarled. "But if these bullies want a fight, then we're going to give them one!"

It was right then that I happened to look up, and I saw something that made my heart skip a beat. Someone was crouched high above us, sitting in the shadows of the many ceiling beams.

It was Ivy.

114:20:12

I BLINKED a few times to make sure I wasn't imagining her, but nope—Ivy was up there, watching and listening. When she saw me looking at her, she held a finger to her lips.

Who *was* this girl—Spider-Man? What was she up to?

Barrington walked to the front of the room. "Next subject: alien spacecraft you might encounter in battle."

Holographic images of weird-looking spaceships hovered a foot above our desks, pulling my attention away from Ivy. The hovering ships kept changing, one example morphing into the next.

"Based on extensive research," Barrington explained, "we've been able to speculate about the array of craft you might be up against."

Speculate? Why didn't he just come right out and say it—he had no idea what we'd be facing.

"The key to victory in any battle is to inflict maximum damage with minimal effort. Hit 'em where it hurts."

Tyler leaned forward, eyes hungrily taking in every inch of the latest ship. It was the most intense and focused I'd seen him so far. Sizing up an enemy was something he'd probably done a million times in his alligator wrestling career.

"Can anyone tell me where you should strike this alien craft?" Barrington asked.

Tyler immediately slouched again as Malcolm began to form an answer.

"I think Tyler might have a good idea, sir," I said.

Tyler's head turned to look at me so fast it was a wonder he didn't snap his neck. His eyes were as wide as frisbees. *This better work,* I thought, *or he's going to break me in half.*

"Well . . . uh . . . ," he began, examining the ship. It was oddly shaped, with two sphere-like sections connected by a thinner section in the middle. "If I had to . . . I'd go for the middle there." He gingerly pointed to it. "It looks like . . . the stomach. And the stomach is always a great weak spot . . ."

Barrington nodded. "That's more or less correct, yes."

Tyler tried to suppress a grin, and I gave him a thumbs-up.

"This sort of spacecraft will most likely have a torque-generating apparatus in its midsection, so a well-delivered strike there will not only sever the ship in two, but also ensure destruction of the remaining halves," Barrington finished.

There was a sudden knock on the door before it opened and Merlin and Pellinore entered. We all sat up straight.

"Knights, I'd like to first apologize for the interruption earlier," Pellinore said to us humbly. "I assure you nothing like that will happen again. My . . . overzealous daughter has been taken home."

I tried to stifle a grin. *That's what you think.* I quickly looked up, but Ivy had vanished.

Pellinore paced along our desks. "Flying in battle requires not only superb hand-eye coordination, but strength and endurance to handle the emotional and physical stress. When you add the rigors of outer space into the mix . . ."

Barrington pressed a panel and the entire back wall split open, revealing a huge observation window. My mouth went dry. Every now and then the scope of our mission would hit me again, like a brick in the face.

Beyond the glass was a massive space, curving hundreds of feet in all directions. There were hundreds of oddly shaped blocks hovering in midair as if weightless, each about the size of a fist. As I took a closer look, I realized they must fit together like puzzle pieces.

"Are we going in there?" I asked breathlessly.

Barrington grinned, those fiery eyes of his flaring to life. "Absolutely."

18

113:56:34

"THE EXERCISE BEGINS . . . *now!"* Barrington's voice boomed into our earpieces.

We had been given custom-fitted silver helmets with built-in communication systems. The platform we stood on suddenly slid forward, delivering us into the zero-g arena. Malcolm leaped up into the air effortlessly as we stopped moving. He somersaulted into a few puzzle pieces, sending them floating off in all directions. Kwan threw himself into the air a split second later and held his arms out as if he was surfing on air. Tyler's bulk worked against him at first, and he looked like he was trying to swim in wet glue. Darla immediately began grabbing puzzle pieces and trying to fit them together.

"Step one, knights. Assemble your keys," Barrington reminded us. Each of us needed to find enough interlocking pieces to make a key that would unlock doors on the other side of the arena. Once past the door, we'd use a gyroscope to steer ourselves back to the landing platform.

My entry into zero gravity wasn't as flashy as the others' by any means. I tried to follow Darla's example, but it was easier said than done. Every time I reached for a piece through my bulky gloves, I'd miss it by inches and fall into a slow-motion somersault.

"Step it up, knights," Barrington warned. "At this rate, the aliens will be here by the time you finish."

Everyone's keys started to take shape, even Tyler's. I was falling further behind. As Darla casually tossed aside extra pieces, they'd float in my direction. I positioned myself so that when her castoffs hit my chest, I could pin them down with my gloves.

"Dude, that's not cool!" Kwan barked. Malcolm, who had been keeping to himself on the other side of the arena, flew past Kwan, holding out his limbs to create an air current in his wake. The pieces floated off with him, leaving Kwan with none. Malcolm began grabbing them and trying to fit them into his key as fast as possible.

As Malcolm continued to float past us, the pieces near us *also* floated off with him. And the tactic was working: His key was soon almost done, and we would have to chase him just for the chance to try more pieces.

But I had an idea. I floated to the wall nearest me, put my feet against it, and propelled myself forward with all I had. As I floated past Darla, I shouted, "Grab on!" and held out a hand for her. "Trust me," I added. "It's the only way!" She hesitated but finally obliged. I wedged my half-completed key under the lip of my helmet, keeping it under my chin so my other hand would be free.

"That way." I pointed to Tyler. He was still moving along the wall, trying to get to more pieces, though there were hardly any left on his side of the arena.

"Tyler, push off the wall as hard as you can as we pass, then take Darla's hand," I instructed.

"NOW!" I yelled as we reached him. His fingertips latched with Darla's at the last second, and Tyler's bulk propelled the three of us forward with even more momentum.

"Kwan, grab my other hand," I called as we passed him. He gave me a glare, but he joined us. With the four of us side by side, we looked like a flying wall. Malcolm, who was now surrounded by the cloud of puzzle pieces, was only one piece away from completing his key.

"Arms out!" I shouted, and Kwan and Tyler extended themselves. As we floated at Malcolm, he had to duck to avoid us. We took all the pieces along with us, leaving Malcolm with none. Then we let go of each other's hands and went back to work.

Darla completed her key first, and a little green light blinked on the end of it. On the opposite wall, a panel slid open to reveal her keyhole. Kwan finished his key next, and then Tyler and I finished ours at almost exactly the same time. More panels slid open. Even Malcolm had quickly caught up and finished his key. We propelled ourselves forward, and all five of us inserted our keys to reveal a gyroscope for each of us. Part two of the race had officially begun.

19

113:35:18

THE GYROSCOPES looked like skeletal twelve-foot-tall spheres: a small steering area at their centers, surrounded by four large steel rings that could spin independently to generate energy.

I climbed into the center of mine and leaned my back against a padded panel. A handlebar apparatus in front of me, similar to the steering mechanism inside X-Calibur, would allow me to launch. I grabbed it and pushed forward. There was a *THWUNK* beneath me, the sound of two metal clasps coming apart to release my gyroscope from its platform. It rolled forward and floated into the arena airspace. I realized quickly that the steering mechanism wasn't there only to steer left or right. I had to use it to keep the sphere balanced, as well, like steering a rowboat on a choppy lake.

I looked to my left and noticed that Malcolm was moving faster than the rest of us, his gyroscope's rings spinning so fast that their blur made me dizzy. Then I saw why. He was pedaling with his feet. I looked down at my own feet and spotted a mechanism similar to the gears of a bicycle. With a determined sneer, I pedaled with all I had, but in my eagerness I leaned too far forward, and my gyroscope almost spun out of control, top over bottom. I barely saved myself from careening off-course. Then I worked on building momentum.

"Yeah, baby! The race is on!" Kwan shouted as the rest of the knights figured out how to make these things fly.

Tyler's beefy legs and arms moved with unbridled power as he grunted and snarled like he was in a fistfight with his gyroscope. He and Malcolm were neck and neck, with Kwan close behind and Darla and me trailing, as all of us headed toward the landing platforms.

BAM! Tyler made it to his platform first, but he was so focused on pedaling like a maniac that he missed his mark and collided with the wall. A second later, Malcolm arrived at his own landing pad perfectly. Surprise, surprise. Malcolm had won.

20

110:51:59

AFTER THE RACE, everyone who worked for the RTR ate in the impressive cafeteria. The tables and chairs were crafted out of sleek steel, the floor was marble, and one entire wall was glass, with a breathtaking (though fake) view of mountains and a lake.

Malcolm assured us that the items in the food line were popular English dishes—stuff like "bangers and mash" (mashed potatoes and sausage), fish-and-chips (French fries), shepherd's pie (*more* mashed potatoes), and black pudding (*more* sausage). With the end of the world upon us, I guess the RTR thought we needed our fill of mashed potatoes and sausage.

"One of everything that doesn't include meat," Tyler ordered the machines serving food. "No, wait—*two* of everything."

"*Why* are you vegetarian again?" Kwan asked, helping himself to a heaping pile of shepherd's pie.

"I respect living things. If you ever wrestle an animal, I bet you'll become a vegetarian, too."

Kwan laughed. "I surf, bro. That's like wrestling the *ocean*. And I still love hamburgers." He turned to me. "Too much of a joke for you, Earnhardt? Are you going to run and tell on me again?"

Tyler sighed. "Leave him alone, Kwan. Ben's cool with me."

I gave Tyler a quick nod as we all sat down, but I felt weird about it. The most important battle mankind has ever faced was approaching, and I couldn't deal with a thirteen-year-old *surfer*? I wondered if King Arthur, Sir Lancelot, and even Pellinore and the rest of the original knights had squabbled like this. I doubted it.

"Nice job flying the gyroscope," I said to Malcolm as our eyes met. I still knew so little about him. A curt nod was all I got in return.

"Do you have experience with that kind of thing?" I wondered.

"What? Preparing to fight aliens?" he asked sarcastically. But then he lightened up a bit. "My family has military experience . . ."

"Indeed they do," Pellinore said as he and Merlin entered the cafeteria. "Going back several generations." He clapped a hand on Malcolm's shoulder, but Malcolm remained strangely quiet.

"Interesting strategy in the zero-g arena, Ben." Pellinore's eyes were on me now. "Unfortunately, if you had been in outer space, you would have gotten yourself, Kwan, Tyler, and Darla killed."

So much for getting a compliment. Kwan and Tyler were staring at me with wide eyes.

"How come?" Darla asked from the end of the table.

"To free up your hands, you put your puzzle keys between your helmet and chin, Benjamin," Merlin explained softly. "That would have breached your helmet's seal. There's no oxygen in outer space. Suffocation is a terribly painful way to expire."

"Now," Pellinore continued. "It's essential that we use the time left to the best of our—" But he stopped when a cluster of techs rushed into the cafeteria, their faces brimming with worry.

"One moment, knights." He and Merlin huddled and whispered with the techs, and we discreetly moved closer. Maybe we didn't get along so great yet, and maybe I had inadvertently "killed" three of them earlier, but we were still in this together.

"What do you think that's about?" Kwan asked Malcolm.

"Can't be sure. But something tells me it's not good," was Malcolm's reply.

We watched as Pellinore gave orders, his expression grim but determined. The techs nodded and rushed out of the cafeteria. Then . . .

BEEP. BEEP. BEEP. BEEP. BEEP.

Five tiny beeps coming from our countdown watches—*nine hours* had been wiped away from the time left until the aliens arrived. Merlin and Pellinore joined us again, eyes wide with new focus.

"Change of plans, knights," Pellinore said urgently, holding out a fist. "Our tracking systems are not without their faults, especially when our targets are still in deep space. Hopefully as our enemies get closer to Earth's atmosphere, these . . . adjustments . . . will be taken care of."

Hopefully?

Merlin added, "We've been forced to speed up our schedule, which means your first foray into our flight simulators will occur immediately. The X-Calibur prototypes, and X-Calibur itself, will follow shortly."

"Come. We're going to the BSR," Pellinore commanded. As we followed, I shot Merlin a questioning glance.

"Battle Simulation Room," he whispered.

21

NOW THAT WE HAD LOST nine hours of prep time, there was an even greater sense of urgency; every second that passed brought us one step closer to sitting behind the controls of X-Calibur.

We quickly arrived at two large doors, which slid open to reveal what looked like nothing—*literally* nothing. No color, no shape, as if someone had taken outer space and then erased every single star. As we stepped into the void, Pellinore pulled a remote control out of his pocket and hit a button. "Let's get you into your training pods," he said.

Five perfectly round pods rose out of the darkness. They weren't very large, maybe five feet across, and practically invisible.

Pellinore pointed to a little microphone on his tie. "My

124

voice will be transmitted to all of you, and, as always, you can speak back to me and each other. An open line of communication will be crucial in battle. Each pod has a different color weapon, so you'll be able to distinguish your own laser fire from everyone else's."

Malcolm quickly headed for one of the pods and slipped through a hatch on its side. Kwan, Tyler, Darla, and I made our way to the remaining four pods, putting on our helmets along the way. With a new sense of dread, I ducked into one, and the hatch swished closed. The inside was cramped, with barely enough space for a pilot seat and steering controls.

"Everyone ready?" Pellinore asked through our helmets. We all quickly chimed in.

"We had planned on Professor Barrington giving you a thorough weaponry tutorial, but with today's . . . developments, the only way to learn is trial by fire."

"Are these lasers real?" I asked, slipping into my seat. "There's no chance we can really hurt each other, right?"

"What makes you think you'll be battling each other?" Pellinore countered. "It is just a simulation. But don't get too comfortable."

As I strapped myself in, he added, "The purpose of this exercise is simple, knights: to make your mistakes now, before you fly an actual craft. Your mission: destroy as many alien ships as possible. And *don't get hit*."

My heart pounded. In the confines of the pod, it

sounded like thunder. I had to push aside the kid I was just a day ago, the one who had to hide inside a smelly gym locker for fear of being pummeled by classmates. I had to find *another* Ben Stone, one who was ready and able to do his part to save the world.

I was pumped and ready. And then . . .

Everything went pitch black. And I mean *everything*.

Except for my steering console and the two floor panels beneath me, which glowed in neon green. I grabbed the controls just as the void outside lit up to reveal a jaw-dropping replication of outer space.

"Bloody brilliant," Malcolm muttered.

My pod began to slowly drift forward, and I felt an instant sense of weightlessness. The experience in the zero-g arena would definitely pay off here.

I spotted something in the distance, and the sight put a lump in my throat. A fleet of alien spaceships, dozens of them, lurked in the distance like a band of metallic sharks. I recognized the shapes from Barrington's lectures.

"Go time," Malcolm hissed, and I watched as a storm of blazing red laser fire blasted out at the approaching aliens. Their sleek sizzle was so real that they blinded me at first. A split second later, yellow, blue, and white lasers cut through the darkness.

I squeezed my weapon triggers, and green lasers rocketed out from beneath my pod. I hadn't been prepared for the sharp kickback from the laser guns, and I was jolted by my pod shuddering. Some of the simulated alien ships exploded on contact with our weapons, disappearing a second later.

Darla is going to kick serious butt at this, I thought. *It's the greatest video game ever.*

The remaining alien ships darted away from each other, and in the blink of an eye there were twice as many of them, coming *at* us now. I yanked to the left and my pod spun sideways. I found myself looking at a whole *other* batch of aliens bearing down on me from *all* directions. Startled, I hammered my laser triggers again. My pod kept shuddering with every blast I unleashed, and I was getting *hit* now too, which was causing my pod to shake even more.

I squinted into the glare of the alien lasers as my mind raced through our previous tests. I felt a bead of sweat rolling down my cheek, the muscles in my arms burning as I tried to hold onto my triggers and control my pod.

"Get outta there, Ben!" Tyler yelled.

"Easier said than done," I grunted.

"Has anybody noticed that I'm kicking *major* butt up here?!" Kwan asked excitedly.

I pulled back on my steering controls as hard as I could, hoping to rise above the storm of alien firepower coming my way. But my right foot hit one of the glowing green panels on the floor. With the sudden surge of juice, the pod began to spin wildly. Dazed, I rolled upside down, then right side up, over and over as I continued to get pummeled. In my panic, I couldn't seem to find the brake.

"No, no, no, no," I chanted, spinning faster and faster. I released the steering controls as my stomach did somersaults and I squeezed my eyes shut. I was in sensory overload, and then . . .

It stopped.

I opened my eyes. The view of space and aliens and everything else had disappeared. The simulation was over.

"Somebody get us more quarters!" Kwan laughed. "Let's go again!"

I took a few steady breaths, fighting back nausea. My pod came to a complete halt as something popped up within my windshield. It was a digital scoreboard with each of the knights' names, kills, and hits taken.

"We've got work to do, knights. Some of you more than others," Pellinore announced.

Malcolm, whose bars were fire-engine red, had clearly done the best. After him came Kwan, then Tyler, then me and Darla in a virtual tie for last place.

"Sweet job, Malcolm," Kwan said. "But I'll get you next time."

"Doubt it," Malcolm replied coolly.

With a groan, I popped open my seat belt, eager to get out of the cramped pod. But as I stood up, my legs felt like melting rubber. I yanked my helmet away from my mouth just in time to double over and hurl chunks right there on the pod floor.

"Oh, man! Call the Keebler elves!" Kwan cried. "Some-body just lost his cookies!"

Everyone had heard.

I closed my eyes and plopped back down into the pilot seat, wishing I were dead.

22

099:13:41

"HEY, WHAT'S Ben's favorite animal?" Kwan asked.

"I don't know. What?" Tyler played along.

"A *yak*." Kwan chuckled. "Get it? It's an animal, but it's also a word for—"

"A joke isn't funny if you have to *explain* it, moron," I griped.

Malcolm led the way back to our rooms, with Kwan and Tyler right behind him. Darla and I followed. Any admiration Kwan had for me was long gone, and I wasn't even sure Tyler thought very highly of me anymore, either.

"What would we call Ben if he had wings and pointy ears and fought crime?" Kwan continued. I answered before he could offer up the punch line himself.

"Barf-man," I said glumly. "Hilarious. We're so lucky

we met the world's only surfer-comedian before we all go ka-boom."

Kwan scowled over his shoulder and kept walking. Darla gave me a tired smirk. She looked drained.

"Are you okay?" I whispered, but she said nothing and looked away. "I thought you would have done better in the pods."

"Hey," she turned on me, her voice low. "You're the one who barfed, remember?"

"Sorry," I muttered.

Ahead of us, Kwan slapped Tyler on the back. "How's it feel to be beaten by someone half your size?"

Tyler shrugged. "I beat you in the jar-a-scope thing, remember? 'Cause I had more room to breathe. Those pods were so tiny."

I looked over at Darla, and a bunch of memories hurtled into my brain: Darla, gazing fearfully down the narrow tunnel at the start of our HQ tour. Darla, lingering at the open door of X-Calibur. The fear in Darla's eyes right before she got into her BSR pod.

"You're claustrophobic, aren't you?" I whispered to her, and the instant panic on her face told me I was right.

She moved closer and grabbed my arm. "Don't tell the others," she pleaded. In front of us, Kwan glanced over his shoulder, so she quickly let go.

"I would *never* tell," I whispered back. "But are you going to be okay in an actual ship?"

She shook her head, flustered. "I don't know. This is all a mistake. I shouldn't be here."

"Why don't we tell Merlin or Pellinore? Maybe they can help you—"

"*No.* Please. They'll send me home. Although, I don't know, maybe they were wrong to bring me here. I'm not cut out for this."

No wonder she'd been keeping to herself. Her shoulders sagged, and for the first time since meeting her, I saw the real Darla.

"I thought I could overcome it at first," she whispered, more to herself than me. "I *wanted* to believe I could be great, but . . . I'm not great. Not at all."

She sounded just like I felt. Video game champion or not, we weren't so different, were we?

"Do your parents know about your . . . problem?" I asked.

"Yeah, but they tell me it's all in my head, that I'm just being weak. Especially my father. He's a *psychologist*," she spat. "He hates video games, and he tries to blame my fear on them."

I nodded sympathetically.

"Forget it, I'm going to tell Pellinore to send me home." She turned to approach the group of techs following us, but I stood in her way.

"Wait," I implored. "Maybe I can find a way for you to overcome your fear."

She looked at me like I was crazy. How the heck was the boy who barfed going to help *anybody*?

"Why do you want to help me so bad?" she countered. "To make sure you won't be the worst knight here?"

"No. I swear. It's just . . . I think . . ." I leaned in and whispered, "We'll need you. Assuming you really are some kind of master shooter."

"What do you mean *assuming*?" she said, shoulders back. "Nobody's better than me at space battle games. You've heard of Astro Galactic Showdown, right?"

"Not really," I admitted.

"Doesn't matter. Point is, I was the first player in the world to ever score ten million points." Her eyes lit up. "It was kind of a big deal. I got an award for it and everything."

"See? That's why we need you," I decided.

She still looked troubled. "What if you're wrong, Ben? This isn't really a time for maybes, is it?"

She was right, of course. But I could ask the same question about myself. I was also one big maybe. "Just give me tonight to think of something," I bargained. "If I can't come up with anything, you can leave tomorrow. Deal?"

She swallowed, but slowly nodded. "Okay. Just tonight."

I looked forward again as we walked on, wondering what the heck I'd just agreed to, and why. What if I somehow got her to stay and then she panicked when the aliens showed up? What if the world ended *because* of Darla? Because *I* had talked her into staying?

Darla reached out to tap my arm. "Hey—even if you can't think of anything, thanks."

I forced a smile, but I couldn't have been more tense. I wasn't making this "defending the world against aliens" thing any easier on myself.

If anything, I just kept making it harder.

23

098:19:10

"I'M THINKIN' I might call home before we go," Tyler said. "What about you, Kwan?"

Back in our room, Malcolm was pulling his sparring outfit out of the closet because he was going to the gym before bed. Tyler and Kwan, both already changed into their sparring outfits, had agreed to go with him. I, however, decided not to join them. I wasn't exactly getting along with any of them, and I still had some lingering nausea from the pod fiasco. I didn't need to risk making a fool of myself again, and I had to figure out how to solve Darla's claustrophobia problem.

"Nah, I'll call later," Kwan replied. "My dad'll just go on and on. As if there aren't more important things to worry about."

"Go on and on about what?" Tyler asked.

135

"My parents want me to quit surfing." Kwan slumped onto the edge of his bed. "They want me to be a doctor or lawyer, but they say that'll never happen if I'm distracted. So they made me promise I'd quit surfing after this year."

"That sucks," I offered, drawn into the conversation from where I was sitting against the wall on my own bed. I thought Kwan might hurl an insult my way, but he didn't.

"Tell me about it." He pulled at the edges of his comforter. "I love surfing, and I'm *good* at it. Plus, I'm not saying I don't want to go to college. I'm just not sure I want to be a doctor or lawyer."

"*I* wanna go to college," Tyler agreed, "but I don't think I can."

"Why not? Too expensive?" I asked.

"That, and I'm just not smart enough for college."

"How do you know if you don't even try?" I countered. "You did just fine in Barrington's class, remember?"

"Yeah, but nobody in my family has gone to college." Tyler let out a loud sigh. "They think since I'm not any smarter than them, it'd be a waste of money."

Kwan rolled his eyes. "That's weak, dude. Sounds to me like they don't *want* you to be smarter than them."

For once, I agreed with Kwan.

Tyler scrunched his face. "Maybe. But we do okay with our croc and gator farm. We're swamped with tourists who wanna see me wrestle."

"So that's what you're going to do for the rest of your

life?" Kwan grimaced. "Wrestle overgrown reptiles while people watch and eat popcorn?"

"My parents didn't go to college either," I offered, "but my mom still wants *me* to go."

"What does she want you to be?" Tyler asked.

"Whatever would make me happy."

Kwan and Tyler paused. "Your mom sounds cool."

I nodded, feeling a little homesick. Malcolm, now sitting on his bed in his jumpsuit, was trying to listen discreetly.

"What do your parents want you to be?" I asked him.

"Well . . . my mother passed away when I was five," he said, averting his gaze.

"Oh. Sorry to hear that." I meant it.

"My father's alive, though," he added.

"Is that his medal you've been carrying around?"

Malcolm reached into his drawer and lifted out the familiar medal. He eyed it a moment, like the sight weighed heavily on him. "My grandfather's. It was awarded to him for outstanding service in the British military. He's a war hero. Legendary in some circles," he said blankly. I remembered a similar expression on his face in the cafeteria when Pellinore said he came from generations of military service.

"Have you called him since you've been here?" I asked.

He shook his head and turned the medal over in his hands. "No use. Gramps is old and doesn't remember much. He has Alzheimer's."

"What about your father? Do you live with him?"

Malcolm tilted his head uncomfortably. He no longer wanted to be in this conversation. "I live with my grandfather, so I can help out when he needs it. My father is a military official, so he travels a lot." He let out a breath and put his grandfather's medal back into the drawer, closing it a little harder than necessary.

"Anyway, I'm going to show a spar-bot who's boss." He turned for the door, and Kwan and Tyler quickly followed.

"Have fun, Earnhardt," Kwan called on the way out. "Don't barf on anything." And then they were gone.

Alone, the room seemed much larger and too quiet. The window screen had paused on a mountain view, and the only sound coming from it was an occasional phony bird chirp. The countdown clock on the opposite wall showed almost ninety-eight hours left until the aliens arrived. I had anxiety in my gut every time I looked at a clock now. It was like being strapped to a ticking bomb.

How the heck can I possibly help Darla? I looked to the window, thinking about how the view tricked our minds, even though it wasn't real. That's when it popped into my head: What if there was a way to trick Darla's brain during battle? I crawled over to the window control panel and pulled it open to look at the guts of the mechanism behind it. A couple of compact wires, probably audio and video, went up and into the wall. I grinned. I had half the puzzle solved . . .

My helmet. Yes! It was on the floor next to my bed. I had a crazy idea. A *ridiculous* idea.

"But it just might work," I whispered.

TWO HOURS LATER, my footsteps echoed as I moved into the gloomy and deserted hallway. I looked out into the dim space to see a light glowing from the ceiling up ahead of me. Waiting. It felt familiar. I had done this before, I remembered, in a dream. I slowly kept walking, and the light suddenly went dark. The one just beyond it then began to glow, waiting for me to continue. I lifted my foot, but hesitated: If I took one more step, something big would happen. I could feel it. But even though my mouth was as dry as chalk and my insides were twisted into nervous pretzels, I had to find out what.

BAM! As my foot hit the floor, it echoed like a bomb detonating. In a flash, I was magnetized to the floor. The hallway took off at a blistering speed, taking me with it. Deeper and deeper into HQ I went, past the room that held the big black box, past the room full of TV screens, until everything around me blurred and I had to close my eyes. All at once, the floor came to a stop. I opened my eyes and looked up at . . . X-Calibur. I had somehow found my way into the underground hangar.

The ship was spotlighted from above, while everything around it was pitch black. I could feel warmth coming from it and hear its gentle hum. I had no idea why I had been brought here, or what I was supposed to do.

The side of the ship shimmered in a pulsing wave of brilliance. I reached out and lay my hand against it. The hum intensified, warmth moving into my hand and up my arm. I should have been afraid, but I wasn't. Not yet.

The ship's surface glistened like water, and the metal began to feel soft against my palm. I pressed into it until my hand went *through* the ship's wall. Then my wrist entered it, then my elbow, as the ship hummed louder, and the warmth crept into my chest. I panicked. I wasn't sure I was ready for this—whatever "this" was—so I tried to pull my arm out of the ship's metallic goo. But something inside X-Calibur *grabbed* me and yanked, my head and shoulders pulled into the swirling metal until—

I woke up in my bed, gasping for air. *Another dream.*

I looked over at the other beds. Malcolm, Kwan, and Tyler slept soundly. I couldn't remember hearing them come back from the gym, but I'd probably passed out in my day clothes and slept through their return. The countdown clock glowed sharply—but then the numbers suddenly disappeared. *What the heck?* Was I dreaming again? I sat up and squinted at the screen.

Letters popped up, one at a time.

B . . . E . . . N . . .

R . . . U . . . AWAKE?

I stifled a cry of confusion.

MEET . . . ME . . . AT . . . THE . . . B . . . S . . . R.

The letters disappeared and the countdown returned, good as new. I pinched myself. Still awake.

Meet me at the BSR.

"Okay," I whispered.

I tiptoed out of bed and into the hall. HQ looked deserted, even though every now and then I could hear voices behind closed doors. I turned a couple of corners, then a couple more, trying to remember how to get to the BSR. It wasn't easy, especially without the luxury of the moving sidewalks to whisk me along.

Eventually I found the place, but I stopped several feet from its doors. I peered suspiciously up and down the halls. This could be some kind of test. Or . . . a trap. There was only one way to find out. I moved in closer.

"They're locked," came a voice from above me. I whirled around, tripped backward, and landed on my butt. I was staring up at Ivy, who was looking down at me from an open ceiling panel.

"What's up?" She grinned. "Besides me, I mean."

"*You* called me on the countdown clock?" I asked in shock. I stood up and brushed myself off hastily.

"Sure. Who else would call you like that?"

Good question.

"How did you, uh, do that?" I asked. She dropped a rope from the open ceiling panel and slid down it effortlessly. She landed beside me with a soft thud.

"I know this place inside and out," she shrugged. "My father brought me here all the time when I was a little kid. I guess he assumed I wouldn't remember it, but I did." She held her chin up. It was the first time I noticed a true resemblance to her father. "I remember *everything*. Plus, I'm pretty good at sneaking around in places I'm not supposed to. It's a gift." She laughed.

I couldn't say anything in return. Now that she was standing in front of me I was distracted by how great she smelled: like flowery apples.

"What's wrong? Cat got your tongue?" she snapped. "Well . . . listen, thanks for not telling my father about me in Barrington's class." She tucked her hair behind her ear and smiled. "That's why I called you here. To say thanks."

"Oh, no prob—" I began, but she held up a finger to cut me off. She'd noticed something down the hall.

"Hold that thought," she said.

She hurried to a hallway door that had light coming from beneath it, then put her ear to the metal. Curious, I made my way over.

"What's going on?" I whispered. I was growing nervous about all this. Not just because Ivy smelled so great and had the greenest eyes I'd ever seen, but also because

142

finding me in the middle of the night with his daughter would give Pellinore a solid reason to kick my scrawny butt back to Texas.

Ivy curled a finger toward the door and carefully opened it. The room looked like an office, with telephones, a copy machine, printers, and a few computers. It was the least amazing room I'd seen at HQ. Ivy pointed to the corner where a tech was bent over a desk, fast asleep, his face sideways on his computer keyboard.

"That's Arlo," Ivy whispered to me with a pitying head shake. "Happens almost every night. My father overworks them," she said regretfully.

As we moved closer, I recognized the tech. He was the flustered, disheveled guy who had delivered the uniforms to our room. As he snored softly, I could see he was definitely much younger than everyone else who worked here, twenty or twenty-one years old at the most.

Ivy watched him sleep, then sighed. She looked around and spotted a jacket draped over another chair, so she grabbed it.

"Lift Arlo's head for me, okay? *Carefully*," she whispered.

I looked over at Arlo doubtfully. "You know, if he wakes up, we're kind of screwed," I said softly. "Should we really even be here?" I'd worked so hard to prove myself here, and I already felt like I was inches away from being kicked out the back door. I didn't want to mess things up any more than I already had.

But Ivy just rolled her eyes. "He's *exhausted*, and even

if he did wake up, he's not going to give us away. We're friends." She brushed off the jacket, looked up at me, and grinned wryly. "You've got to have a little faith, Ben."

I sighed, grabbed Arlo's head, and lifted his cheek off the keyboard.

"Move him to the right," Ivy whispered, and I did. The chair swiveled to help me. Ivy folded up the jacket like a pillow and placed it on the desk, next to the keyboard.

"Okay, put him down."

I did, with his cheek on the folded jacket. He stirred briefly, then resumed his slumber. Ivy gave me a smile. "Better. If he slept on the keyboard all night, his cheek would look like a waffle in the morning."

We made our way back into the hall and closed the door.

I pointed to the open ceiling panel with the rope still hanging down. "Aren't you afraid someone'll see that?"

"Nah. Things are on a pretty set schedule around here at night. There's usually no one walking the halls for another five hours."

"Do you live here or something? Your dad said you were taken home."

She walked over to the rope as I followed.

"My father is so focused on his work that it's easy to pull one over on him. *Too* easy, actually. But no, technically I don't live here."

"Technically?"

She contemplated whether or not to tell me more. Those blazing green eyes of hers locked on mine, her expression firm. "I'll show you. But it's top secret, okay? Under normal circumstances—like if the world wasn't potentially going to end—I'd have to kill you afterward." She smirked and grabbed the rope. "Follow me."

I began to climb. The ceiling was only twelve feet high, so thankfully I didn't have far to go. But a foot away from the ceiling, my arms trembled under the strain. I had an empty stomach, so I was even weaker than usual. I reached up to grab the edge of the open panel, but instead of grabbing metal, I grabbed Ivy's *hand*. She had gotten down on her stomach to help me up with a grunt.

"Thanks," I panted, and climbed into the ceiling. She yanked the rope up and put the panel back in place.

The inside of the ceiling was only lit through thin slits in the paneling. It took a moment for my eyes to adjust. Everything was a dizzying network of steel beams and pipes and wires, the guts of this amazing HQ. It was like being inside a massive machine.

"Now what?" I whispered.

Ivy pointed up. I tilted my head back for a look at ladder rungs that had been bolted to the side of a steel beam.

"What's up there?"

"My home away from home." Then she was off again, climbing higher and higher into the darkness.

"Note to self," I muttered. "Next time someone calls me on a countdown clock, don't answer." I grabbed the first ladder rung and began to climb.

25

IVY HIT THE SWITCH on a power strip, and two small lamps came on with a soft click. The floor we stood on was a solid sheet of metal that stretched as far as I could see. It had a slight curve to it, bending down at the edges, like we were standing atop an enormous ball.

I cautiously stepped forward. "Are we on top of the zero-g arena?"

"It's the top of the BSR," Ivy corrected me. "But the construction is similar."

I looked up at the intersecting beams and wires and pipes, which also stretched as far as I could see. The inner workings of HQ seemed to go on for miles.

"Are you hungry?" Ivy walked over to the nest of her things: a sleeping bag, headphones, a few bottles of water, a laptop, and a backpack and duffel bag.

146

"A little, yeah." I was starving.

"Help yourself." She tossed me the backpack, hard, and I wasn't quite ready for it. It practically knocked me over, but I tried to look casual. Inside was everything from potato chips to candy to brownies wrapped in plastic.

"Try the brownies," Ivy suggested. "Emma made them. They're fantastic."

"Emma?"

"The woman who watches me. At home."

Emma isn't doing a very good job, I thought.

I bit into one of the brownies. My stomach, which had been growling a moment ago, was now doing backflips and screaming for more.

"Wow," I mumbled through a full mouth. "These *are* good."

"Have all you want. I've got plenty. Water?"

Before I could answer, she hurled a bottled water my way. I barely stopped it from taking off half my face. As I ate, Ivy sat down on her sleeping bag and opened her laptop. I walked over and kneeled a few inches from the sleeping bag, keeping my distance. She glanced my way, considered me for a moment, then went back to her laptop.

"I picked this spot because the Wi-Fi signal is strongest here. Download speeds off the charts," she explained, typing away.

I fumbled for something to say. "I uh, think the coffee shop where I live is getting Wi-Fi soon."

"Oh, yeah? Starbucks?"

I shook my head.

"Coffee Bean?"

"No. Joe's Coffee." I wiped a chocolate smudge on my shirt.

"Hmm. I've never heard of that one."

"The guy who owns it is named Joe."

She smiled as if I were joking, but when I didn't smile back, she murmured "oh" and went back to her screen. To her left I noticed a green iPod.

"That's an old one," she said when she saw me eyeing it. "I use it up here so if it falls over the side and breaks, I won't miss it."

"But it looks brand new," I said, leaning in for a closer look.

She handed it to me. "It's nine months old. They make a much better one now. I have a couple of them at home. I usually listen to music on my iPad or iPhone now, anyway."

"Sure. Makes sense," I muttered, eyeing the iPod. My parents had planned to buy me a *used* iPod for Christmas the year before Dad died, but by the time they went to Smiley's Pawn Shop, someone else had offered a better price for it.

"What do you like to listen to?" she asked.

"Mostly CDs." I couldn't look Ivy in the eye because I was remembering the sound of Dad singing in the mirror each day before work.

"You can have that iPod if you want it." She said it like she was offering me a potato chip. But I handed it back to her.

"That's okay, but thanks. I will take a second brownie, though." I dug into another delicious mouthful. "Does your mom cook too?"

Ivy scoffed. "No way. Mother's skills are going on exotic vacations and spending insane amounts of money."

"Like family vacations?" I couldn't wrap my head around the idea of Percival Pellinore sitting on a beach and sipping a drink with a little paper umbrella in it.

"No. My parents are separated."

"Is that like . . . divorced?"

"They might as well be." Ivy sighed. "Do you know my father never even intended to tell me he was *the* Percival Pellinore? I only found out because I spied on him and my mother when they had *the* conversation."

"What's *the* conversation?"

"The one where he told her he'd been alive for hundreds of years already. You should have seen her face." Ivy gave a harsh laugh and pushed the laptop away. "She was ready to have him hauled off to the loony bin. But then he proved it to her. He had everything ready—documents, photos. It's funny, it would be so simple for just about anyone to discover who he really is, but nobody would ever believe it. He can hide out in the open."

At least Pellinore was trying to do something good with all his money and power, and I respected that. He'd give anything to protect Earth.

"If my father had his way, I'd be locked in a stone tower like some fairy tale. It's maddening. Just because he's

149

immortal doesn't mean I am. I've got one *normal* life. I think I should be allowed to make the most of it, don't you?"

"Totally." I nodded, then leaned back on my hands, getting comfortable. I had forgotten all about our amazing surroundings. The endless pipes, the top of the BSR sphere, all of it. All that mattered was Ivy.

"By the way, I thought it was big of you to call Kwan out earlier for not taking all this seriously. And how you pushed Tyler to participate in class, too. He's not Einstein, but he's got more smarts than he gives himself credit for," Ivy said with a little smile.

"Thanks." My cheeks got warm.

She nodded to her laptop. "I know everything there is to know about Tyler. And Kwan, and Darla, and Malcolm, too. I've been hacking into my father's secret files for years. If he knows it, I know it. *You're* the only one who's still a mystery. Because Merlin brought you here."

"I guess I'm just not sure *why* Merlin picked me. If you've read about the other knights, then you already know they've been . . . special. Champions at something. And Malcolm . . ." I just shook my head, unable (or unwilling) to put Malcolm's apparent greatness into words.

Ivy held up a hand. "You don't have to say a thing about Malcolm, believe me. All the girls at the school we attend think he's the greatest thing since popcorn."

"But you don't?" I dared to ask.

She reached for a chip and popped it in her mouth with

a satisfied crunch. "He's a little too . . . serious. I suppose I respect him more than I like him."

I couldn't suppress a tiny grin. But she was staring at me again, trying to figure me out. I wondered if I was here, in her "home away from home," because I was the only mystery left for her to solve.

She shrugged. "Anyway, I'm sure Merlin had his reasons for bringing you here. Don't pull a Tyler and sell yourself short, okay? You do that and you're sure to fail miserably."

I nodded. "Thanks. I better go back now, though. Your dad's having us fly the prototypes soon."

"I know. It's been pushed back," she said, pointing to a schedule on the laptop. "Something about the training course needing a few more obstacles."

I headed to the ladder but stopped. "You're already a pro up there. Any flying tips?" I hoped.

"Yeah. Never forget that your brain can do several things at once if you allow it to. You've got to trust your mind. Don't strangle whatever skills you have by getting too worked up over any one detail."

"So you're telling me not to *think* too much, huh?"

She smiled. "Exactly. And whatever you do, keep your steering measured and controlled, or you'll find yourself in a spin. I'm going to assume you're not interested in vomiting again."

I winced. "You saw that?"

"I heard it. I was listening in on the comm system channel."

She performed an unflattering impression of me right before I puked—"No, no, no, no . . ."—then punctuated it with a "SPLAT!"

"Very funny." I scowled, and we both laughed. "You know, it's crazy you're not going to be flying a ship," I added.

The look in her eyes was heartbreaking. "Princess in a stone tower," she said softly. "That's me."

26

087:52:19

JUST AS IVY had predicted, we woke up to the news that we'd be flying the prototypes later than expected. After a quick breakfast from Arlo's food cart (a single bowl of cornflakes, in case I managed to make myself nauseated again), we headed to the gym and trained while waiting for Merlin and Pellinore to take us to the ships.

Before long, I was getting my butt handed to me by a spar-bot. Earlier, Darla and I had secretly switched training helmets with each other. When she saw all of the adjustments I'd made to the inside of mine last night, she'd looked downright scared.

"How is this going to help me?" she'd whispered frantically.

"I'll explain later," I promised. "You just have to trust me."

WHAM! The spar-bot bearing down on me whacked me

in the ribs with its sword, its blue eyes aglow with a burning desire to *destroy me*. Even though my sparring outfit was padded, the blow still knocked the wind out of me.

"You really have some anger issues," I grunted, then swung back with both hands on my sword handle. The overgrown toaster easily dodged the swing and whacked me in my *other* side. I gasped as spittle flew out of my mouth.

Malcolm and his spar-bot were moving about the gym as they traded impressive sword moves. Did I regret spending time with Ivy last night instead of practicing in here with the other knights? Nope. But it still sucked playing catch-up, especially when it meant the rest of the knights got to watch me cower in the corner while a spar-bot practically beat me to death with a fake sword.

"New strategy!" I shouted. I dropped to my knees and scrambled between the spar-bot's legs, emerging on the other side and running off. The shiny warrior whirled, its lighted eyes piercing.

"You're supposed to fight it, Earnhardt!" Kwan yelled with a chuckle. "Not play hide-and-seek with it!"

As I ran across the gym, I could feel my sparring outfit sticking to me, my entire body coated in sweat. Sword *running* was apparently even more of a workout than sword-*fighting*. I reached the opposite wall and turned to see my spar-bot charging at me like some crazed Energizer bunny.

"Don't sell yourself short," I muttered to myself as the spar-bot came at me.

WHOOSH! The spar-bot swung the sword in a wide

uppercut, but I dodged to my right and it missed me. Thrilled and surprised, I turned, raised my sword, and— *WHAM!*—struck the spar-bot's back. There was an electronic *buh-bloop* as I finally scored some points against it.

"You want some more?" I challenged, but the spar-bot spun low and hit me behind the knees. I went flying backward and landed on my back with a jarring thud, gasping for breath.

"Ugh. I think I just popped a lung," I wheezed.

As I looked up into the glowing stare of my triumphant opponent, it gently put one metallic knee on my chest and stuck the tip of its sword against my throat.

"I win," it said flatly. It almost sounded like a computerized version of Pellinore.

"Rematch?" I gulped. The spar-bot hesitated, its sword still at my throat.

"I accept," it replied and stood.

"Lucky me," I groaned. I pulled myself up for another go, but the gym's door opened and Pellinore entered, crisply dressed as always, with Merlin right behind him in brown corduroy pants and a long-sleeved thermal shirt that emphasized his scrawniness.

"Who's ready to pilot an actual ship?" Pellinore asked.

"I am, sir!" Malcolm called back. I glanced at Merlin and he gave me a nod. Even after the barf fiasco in the BSR, he still seemed to believe in me.

"Me too," I told Pellinore as I stepped forward.

"No more accidents, I hope?" he asked me sternly.

I fought back a blush and tried my best impression of Malcolm. "No, sir! All good! I only had one bowl of cereal for breakfast! Sir!"

Merlin smirked while Malcolm scrunched his nose and Pellinore eyed me like I'd lost my mind.

"Very well. Get into your training jumpsuits and grab your helmets, knights. Let's go do some flying."

27

086:22:34

LINED UP by the four X-Calibur imitations, holding our helmets and buzzing with adrenaline, we prepared to finally try what we'd been brought here to do: fly. A million thoughts raced through my head as I tried to give Darla a reassuring smile. She was nervously clutching the helmet I had given her. Was I delusional to help her? What if my helmet adjustments didn't work, and she crashed in front of us all? Were we really ready for this?

Stop thinking so much.

"We're going to get you airborne two at a time," Pellinore explained. Then he and Merlin stood aside to let Professor Barrington take the lead.

"Once the first two prove capable of handling their spacecraft, we'll put the second two up," Barrington growled, chewing on his trusty nail. "Your goal is to fly laps. Nothing more."

"I've had the techs install temporary guards over the laser triggers, so firing won't be an option for you, anyway," Pellinore added.

"What about X-Calibur?" Malcolm asked. "Who gets to fly that?"

"No one—" Merlin began, but Pellinore interrupted him.

"*Not yet.* But prove yourself worthy, Malcolm, and X-Calibur will be yours soon enough."

"If we go up in pairs, that'll leave someone out, right?" Kwan asked. "There's five of us, and only four ships."

Pellinore nodded and was about to answer when Darla suddenly offered, "*I* can go last."

We all turned to look at her, and I spotted disappointment on Pellinore's face. The last thing he wanted was a kid who didn't want to be here. Darla was only drawing more attention to herself, and if my helmet trick was going to work, we needed to keep it under the radar.

"If that makes things easier, I mean," Darla added uncertainly.

"Ben and I can go up together," said Malcolm. "If that's okay with him, of course."

He wasn't wasting any time trying to make sure I looked worse than I already did.

"Of course it's okay," I said firmly. "I'm ready."

"Excellent!" Pellinore declared. "After that you'll be joined in the air by Kwan and Tyler."

Kwan slapped Tyler on the back. "Booyah!"

Pellinore gave a curt cough and continued. *"Then,* one of you will swap out with Darla."

"I'll swap with her after I get my chance to fly," Malcolm offered. *Seriously?* I guess he figured it wouldn't take long for him to make me look stupid up there. I thought I might barf again.

A few minutes later, I strapped myself into my pilot seat. Even though the RTR's engineers had done an impressive job of replicating the one-of-a-kind alien ship, there were still some differences between X-Calibur and the proto-types, like the amount of space inside the ship's cabin. There was barely two feet on either side of me; the walls of the prototype were thicker and bulkier than I had expected.

I grabbed the ship's steering handlebars, and the pro-totype hummed with power as it came to life. Through the windshield I could see Merlin, Pellinore, Barrington, Darla, Kwan, and Tyler watching.

"Can you hear me, knights?" Pellinore asked through our helmets.

"Ready when you are," Malcolm said.

"You may begin," Pellinore advised, and my ship be-gan to rumble from the thrusters below.

I pulled back on my steering handlebars (slowly, *mea-sured,* like Ivy had advised) and my ship hummed louder and the front end began to rise.

"You're going to need some thrust, Benjamin," Merlin suggested.

I put my foot on the floor panel labeled THRUST. It glowed as I made contact with it, but I hit it too hard and my ship suddenly rose straight up, *fast*, headed toward the ceiling. I would smash into it in about two seconds flat and die a very moronic death if I didn't do something. I panicked, and then it occurred to me to simply *take my foot off the thrust panel.*

Whew. I was now hovering in place, with Malcolm's ship only thirty feet away. Every few seconds, I gave my ship some gentle power to keep it afloat.

"Release the lap markers," Pellinore ordered. I looked down through my windshield and saw a couple of techs carrying a remote-control unit with buttons on it. Panels in the hangar's ceiling suddenly slid open, and a few dozen orange glowing pyramids, each about six feet long, descended on gleaming silver chains. As they settled into their positions, they transformed the hangar airspace into a circular flying racetrack. The hangar lights dimmed, and the pyramids cast an eerie orange haze over the entire place. It would have been cool if I hadn't been so darn nervous.

"This should be fun," I muttered, then took a deep breath.

"The course is all yours, knights," Pellinore prompted. In the blink of an eye, the back end of Malcolm's ship lit up with a surge of power, and he soared forward. Even though we were just supposed to fly laps, Malcolm was going to turn this into a race.

I gave my ship some power and moved forward, much slower than Malcolm. I just wanted to avoid the glowing pyramids, and I did a pretty good job. Problem was, I looked like a grandma driving a Ferrari. I wasn't going to impress anyone at this speed, and when I saw Malcolm whizzing around the opposite side of the hangar, I knew I had to kick it up a notch.

I gave my ship more juice, and the engines roared behind me like a barely contained inferno. Warmth from the fire spread through the cabin. With my sweaty hands clutching the steering controls in a death grip, I left my doubts behind and focused everything I had on keeping the ship on course.

Ivy was right. I can do this!

I was jolted by something surging past my windshield: Malcolm had lapped me. I squinted into the fiery red of his rear thrusters as he left me in the dust. So much for my awesomeness.

"Nice work, Malcolm," Pellinore cheered. I wished Ivy was here to fly a ship and give Malcolm a run for his money.

"Okay, you two—Kwan and Tyler are on their way up now," Barrington warned. "Stay sharp and remember: Communication is key. Talk to each other up there. You're a team."

Tell that to Malcolm.

I looked around, trying to spot Tyler and Kwan. They suddenly appeared on either side of me. Even though their ships were at least twenty feet away, I felt nervous again.

The seat belt that was crisscrossed over my chest was tight, making me aware of every inhale and exhale, not to mention my galloping heart.

"Eat my dust," Kwan jeered. His ship rocketed forward and clipped a couple of the course markers, which swung on their chains like pendulums. One of them almost hit me, but I avoided it by inches.

KA-WHOOOSHH!! I soared around a corner and accelerated into a straightaway, gaining some confidence again. The control over the spacecraft was exhilarating. I would have given anything to have Mom there to see me. Or Dad.

THWUNK. I heard something collide with something else behind me. I tried to turn in my seat, but couldn't see what it was.

"Everybody okay? I heard something," I asked.

"It was me," Tyler responded. "I hit one of those glowing things. But I'm okay."

"What are you doing up there?" Barrington snarled over the comm system. "You've got eighty feet of vertical airspace, and you're clustered together like a bunch of daisies!"

There was a roar above me as Malcolm suddenly rose higher. Kwan or Tyler also vanished.

"Kwan," I called. "You high or low?"

"Low."

I looked down at my feet. I didn't like that idea; he already seemed like a loose cannon as a pilot. Since Malcolm must have been way above me, I pulled back on my steering controls to give Kwan more room.

"Whoa!! Watch it, Earnhardt!" Kwan suddenly screamed. Then I looked around and my eyes widened. His ship was probably a foot above me. We were practically touching each other!

"You said you were low!" I hissed.

"I am low!"

"Then why are you *above* me?!"

"I meant I'm lower than *Malcolm*!" my earpiece crackled.

"How is that supposed to help me?"

"I don't know! You're the one who asked!" His ship teetered slightly from side to side.

I was starting to get a bad feeling about this flight.

"Where's Tyler?" I asked warily.

"I'm also lower, Ben," he answered.

"Lower than *what*?"

"Malcolm. Well, you too, of course."

What? I yanked the controls to avoid crashing into Tyler and maneuvered left, *hard*. I surged completely off-course and through the middle of the hangar. Even worse, in my panic my knee smacked into the underside of the ship's handlebars, and I heard something knock loose on the console.

When I grabbed the controls with both hands again to stop my ship from twirling, my thumb accidentally pressed the laser trigger and—

KA-SWISH!! I'd knocked the trigger guard loose, and now the hangar lit up like the Fourth of July as a laser blasted out of my ship! It crackled like a bolt of lightning as it tore straight through one of the hanging pyramids, blasting it to smithereens, the pieces soaring through the air like glowing rocks.

The laser kept going until it tore into the far wall, and a large slab tumbled down. In disbelief, I watched as it plummeted straight toward Merlin, Pellinore, Barrington, Darla, and the techs. Six people, two of them bona fide historical legends, were moments away from being crushed like ants.

All because of me.

085:36:17

TIME STOOD STILL as I watched the massive piece of wall plummet. Without thinking, I grabbed the plastic guard of my ship's other laser trigger and pulled it so hard that it broke in half. I wrapped both hands around my controls. Blasting apart the falling piece of wall would be the only way to save everyone down there, *if* I could obliterate it while it was still falling.

KA-SWISH! SWISH! Suddenly, two lasers, one right after the other, pierced through the darkened hangar and rocketed toward the piece of falling wall.

Malcolm.

He apparently had the same idea as me, and his lasers destroyed the slab in midair. Everyone below covered their heads as they were showered with pebbles, but nobody was harmed. Malcolm saved the day, but not from evil aliens; he had saved it from me.

I slammed my foot on my deceleration panel and whipped around just in time to avoid another wall. When I was sure I was far enough away from anything else dangerous, I took a stab at landing. I managed to get back on the ground without blowing myself up, although it wasn't the smoothest landing in history, that's for sure.

I paused to catch my breath, dreading what would come next. Would I be sent home after this debacle? When I finally got out of my ship, the first face I noticed in the dusty haze was Darla's. She shot me a questioning look, then glanced down at her helmet, as if to ask if I'd done all this on purpose. Did she think I'd planned to bury her under two tons of concrete?

"It was an accident," I breathed. I flashed back to Pellinore lecturing me in the gym about not having any more accidents. I was pretty sure he would have traded a little barf for this mess right now.

"The trigger guard broke off. My knee hit it," I explained sheepishly.

Barrington was staring at me, lip curled, his shaved head speckled with tiny pieces of concrete and plaster.

"And the firing?" Pellinore asked me pointedly, shaking similar dust from his hair. He looked like he'd just come from a snowstorm.

"Also an accident," I muttered, but no one was listening, because Malcolm had landed and was headed this way.

"Malcolm, thank you!" Pellinore gushed and gave him a warm handshake. "We owe you our lives."

"Just doing my job, sir."

Merlin stepped forward. "Fine work, Malcolm. Fine work, indeed."

I looked away, ashamed. Tyler and Kwan had messed up too, but at the end of the day, I had blown apart a wall. Behind us, the sounds of Kwan and Tyler landing with clunky thuds echoed across the hangar. The two of them jumped out of their ships and came over to us.

"Did you see me up there?" Kwan shouted happily. "I totally rule at flying!" He turned to me and scowled. "But what's the deal with the shooting, Earnhardt? Kinda dangerous, don't you think?"

"*Accident*," I grunted through clenched teeth.

"When can we fly again?" Tyler asked.

Pellinore surveyed the debris, then the damaged wall. "We'll need to get this cleaned up and make sure the hangar is structurally sound first. We're three hundred feet below ground. It won't do mankind any good if we're all buried alive."

"I'm sorry," I croaked. The words sounded incredibly tiny in this vast space. I looked at Merlin, because most of all I was sorry to him. But he looked away.

"I need the bathroom," I said. I needed to be alone, and honestly, almost killing six people does strange things to your bladder.

Pellinore wagged a hand toward the door, like he

wanted to sweep me right out of here and back to Texas. "Go."

Five minutes later, I was still standing in a bathroom stall, eyes closed. My attempt to find peace was interrupted by a muffled sound. A door slammed somewhere in another nearby room. And then, two voices: Pellinore's and Merlin's. I looked up and spotted a heating vent in the ceiling.

With nothing to lose, I climbed onto the back of the toilet and stretched closer to the vent. The voices were louder now. I stood on my toes and pushed aside the vent cover. There was a metal beam running across the exposed space. I grabbed the beam and tried to pull myself up. I flailed back and forth until I had the momentum to swing my legs up and over one of the stall walls. I pulled and pushed myself into the open ceiling—Ivy would have been impressed.

Holding my breath, I crawled through the cramped space, following the sound of their voices. The network of beams and pipes was dense here, not giving me much wiggle room. But I soon looked down through another heating vent to see Merlin and Pellinore in a room that looked like Pellinore's office. They stood beside shiny metal bookcases, across from an ancient-looking tapestry with crossed swords.

"I have immense respect for you, Merlin, you know that," Pellinore was saying.

"But?" Merlin prompted, standing before him.

"You're misguided. That boy does not have knight potential."

That boy. Pellinore couldn't even bring himself to say my name. Even worse, Merlin apparently didn't have an argument to defend me.

Merlin pressed a hand to his forehead warily. "Let's talk about Ivy, then," Merlin replied. My eyes widened.

"Please, not again—" Pellinore protested, but Merlin held up his free hand and silenced him. It was weird to see someone who looked like a kid put a big, confident guy like Percival Pellinore in his place.

"If anything, this mishap has proven how much we need her," Merlin began. "And need I remind you that we wouldn't even have a chance of using X-Calibur against the coming extraterrestrials if it wasn't for Ivy?"

Pellinore lowered his head as if he couldn't keep it up any longer under the weight of everything. "You're not telling me anything I don't already know," he admitted.

"I know how much you care for her, but when it comes to your daughter, you wear blinders," Merlin chided him.

Pellinore looked up again, pleading. "She's my only child, Merlin. I've watched so many people I care about come and go. I've outlived them all—"

"As have I," Merlin interrupted.

"—but never my own flesh and blood. I resisted getting too close to anyone after our brothers in the knighthood died. It was only after Ivy's birth that I understood the joys of family again. They are beyond compare, old friend."

Pellinore's face clenched. Seeing how much he cared about Ivy made me miss my father even more than I already did.

"If we fail, and if our knights cannot rise to the challenge, then we're all dead," Merlin reasoned. "And no amount of love will be able to save her then. Or anyone else."

I held my breath as I waited for him to say something. I heard a toilet flush behind me. Someone was in the bathroom, and I had left the ceiling panel open! Panicked, I scrambled back the way I had come as quietly as possible. When I got to the open panel over the bathroom stall, I lowered myself through it.

SPLASH! My feet landed in the toilet. I lost my balance and fell backward, toward the stall door, hitting it with my head. It flew open and I hit the bathroom floor on my back, my sopping wet shoes now propped up on the toilet rim. If that wasn't bad enough, I looked up at . . . Malcolm.

He crossed his arms. "This is odd," he said, deadpan. "Although I'm beginning to think odd is your middle name."

"I, uh, heard something in the ceiling. A rat. I was trying to catch it. They carry diseases, you know."

He rolled his eyes and extended a hand, so I took it and stumbled to my feet.

"Thanks. Not just for that, but for, you know, saving everyone. I don't know what I would've done if they—"

"Just be more careful next time, okay?" he said, his tone softening a bit. I think he had finally concluded that I was zero competition for him.

"I'm trying, believe me."

He eyed me a moment. "Look, we all know Merlin brought you here."

I nodded. "Yeah?"

"Well . . . being like that . . . it probably messes with him, don't you think?"

"Being like what?" I asked.

"Aging backward. Who knows what that does to a bloke's mind." Malcolm's lips thinned into a stiff line.

We were both suddenly startled by the sound of Pellinore shouting out in the hall. When Malcolm and I joined everyone in the atrium, there were whispers among the techs that Pellinore had an important announcement. Merlin spotted me, then looked to my shoes. They were dripping wet, creating a puddle of toilet water around me.

"I can explain," I whispered, but he held up a hand. The stress of championing me had probably aged him a couple of months backward already.

When everyone finished gathering, Pellinore stood before us, and, to my surprise, I realized *Ivy* was next to him.

"For those of you who don't already know her," Pellinore began, "this is my daughter, Ivy." He took a deep breath. "From now on . . . she'll be a part of our team."

Ivy was glowing at the news. I've never seen someone look happier, and I couldn't have been happier *for* her. We even shared a knowing smile.

"Not only will Ivy be a potential prototype pilot," Pellinore continued, "but she'll also be in contention for the honor of . . . flying X-Calibur."

I looked over at Malcolm. His jaw was clenched, genuinely intimidated. I'm not going to lie—I loved it.

"However, in light of the fact that we now have five ships and six pilots, our plans will have to be altered somewhat," Pellinore added. "Knights, in only a short time, one of you will be *cut* from this mission, and your knighthood terminated."

Gulps all around. "Who's going to be cut?" Darla asked. She was still clutching the helmet I had given her, like it was a life preserver.

"That remains to be seen," Pellinore replied, though he glanced in my direction.

"Can't you just build another ship?" Kwan asked.

Pellinore sighed. "Each of our four X-Calibur prototypes took sixteen years to build. None of the others are even *close* to ready. To put it bluntly, this is now survival of the fittest. Show us what you've got—or go home."

29

084:10:08

WE WERE ALL in the cafeteria again, and the tension in the air among the six potential knights was so thick you'd need a chain saw to cut it. Twenty minutes ago, even with my screw-ups, it wasn't like there was another kid here ready to take my place. But not anymore. Now, either Darla or I would probably go home.

Kwan, Tyler, and Malcolm kept stealing awkward glances at Ivy, who sat by us, eating quietly. I felt bad for her. She knew this HQ better than anyone, but she was still an intruder in our group. Malcolm seemed especially uptight. He was pushing his food around his plate while he tried to figure out just how worried he needed to be.

Darla was the only one who wasn't concerned. She was seated at the end of the table, closest to the large window, with my helmet next to her. What if it allowed her to

173

overcome her claustrophobia and kick butt? That would probably seal my fate here, and I'd be saying sayonara.

"How's your lunch, Ben?" Ivy suddenly asked me from across the table, and the eyes of Kwan, Tyler, and Malcolm immediately darted toward me. I swallowed.

"Fine," I mumbled, "just fine." Then l looked down at my plate and resumed chewing. So did everyone else. I didn't want to let on that Ivy and I had already hung out. It would definitely bring up questions and suspicions, especially from Malcolm, and I had enough to worry about.

After a few seconds, I glanced at Ivy, but the disappointment in her eyes over my sudden coldness was clear. This sucked. We were supposed to be a team, not competitors who ate in silence. I was about to open my mouth and apologize to her when I spotted Pellinore heading our way.

"Knights, my techs have informed me that it's going to take longer than expected to repair the hangar. In the meantime, let's get all of you in the BSR pods again."

"Make sure Earnhardt takes the same pod he had last time!" Kwan shouted as we entered the BSR. "No way *I'm* takin' the one he yakked in!"

Pellinore and Merlin walked into the BSR with us. The massive space was free of any stars. I looked up, trying to see the curved ceiling as I remembered standing on top of it with Ivy.

"Since there are six of you now, to keep it fair we think

174

it's best to have you compete three at a time. The first three up will be Ben, Darla, and Ivy," Pellinore declared.

Ivy only met my eyes for a split second before turning away coldly and walking confidently to her pod. She was still angry with me for blowing her off in the cafeteria. I tried to walk with her, but Darla hurried up alongside me, whispering frantically. "What do I do with this helmet, Ben? Please—"

"I set it up to tap into the power of the helmet's comm system," I quickly whispered back. "As soon as Pellinore turns on his microphone to talk to us, it'll fire it up."

"Fire *what* up? You have to show me," she pleaded.

"Okay. *Quick*," I relented, and we both climbed into her pod. It was impossibly cramped with both of us in there, and her eyes went wide with fear.

"Oh, no, no, no," she gasped, hyperventilating. "I c-can't do this!"

She was practically shivering with panic, and I thought, *This is a huge mistake. I should have let her quit already.* But it was too late to go back now—why not at least give my helmet a try?

"Yes, you can, Darla. Sit down and close your eyes. You have to trust me."

I turned over the helmet to examine the tiny window scenery device I had put in there. I had attached its video wire to the helmet's glass with a couple of Band-Aids I'd found in our bathroom.

175

"What's going on in there, Ben and Darla?" Pellinore barked over the comm system. Now that the helmet's power had been initiated, the little scenery unit lit up. It was working!

I quickly put on the helmet to see how it looked. I gasped; it was better than I could have even imagined. The helmet's glass now had a wide-open mountain view on it, just like the one in the room window or cafeteria. The image was slightly transparent. There was a lake at the base of the mountain, and I could look through the water to the pod's windshield. It was like being in two worlds at once.

I yanked the helmet off and gave it to Darla. "Here! Put it on and you'll see!" I whispered, putting a finger to my mouth, reminding her to keep her voice down. Whoever else was on the comm line might hear us now. Her entire body relaxed as she gazed through the helmet's glass. She didn't need to say a thing. The trick had fooled her brain into thinking she was somewhere other than a cramped pod.

She pulled off the helmet. "How can I ever repay you?" she whispered.

"Just do great," was my answer. And I meant it. I turned to climb out of the pod, but then I stopped and turned back.

"Actually, there is something," I said quickly. "You're a girl, right, Darla?"

"Last I checked, yeah."

I scratched the back of my neck awkwardly. "Well . . . I snuck out of the room last night with Ivy."

Darla's eyes widened in surprise. "It was her idea," I added quickly. "She called me to come and meet her. My question is: Why would she do that? I think she's mad at me now, and I'm not sure what to do."

Darla just smiled a little.

"What?" I asked defensively.

"Well, for someone who's obviously so smart"—she nodded to the helmet—"you sure sound dumb as a skunk right now. Just tell Ivy how you feel. Tell her you're sorry. Just . . . be you. She obviously already likes you, Ben."

I smiled, feeling pretty dumb, even though I was glad I asked. "Thanks."

I squeezed out of the pod. "Sorry, Mr. Pellinore! Everything's fine! Darla just needed help with her seat belt."

Before they could ask questions, I climbed into my pod, put on my helmet, and took a few quick, deep breaths.

Show us what you've got or go home, Pellinore had said.

"Sounds like a plan," I muttered. "Bring on the fake aliens."

30

076:03:23

THE GOOD NEWS was that I didn't get any more motion sickness during the first round of BSR training against Ivy and Darla. The bad news: I came in third place.

Ivy won, but with Darla's claustrophobia under control, she was finally able to use her video game skills. In the second round, Malcolm won easily, but everyone was getting better. We trained for *hours,* always switching up the participants. The most exciting rounds were the ones with Malcolm and Ivy. He won the vast majority of them, though Ivy did beat him a couple of times and came close on all the others. Pellinore never once praised his daughter.

When the day-long BSR-fest finally ended, there was no way to sugarcoat the outcome. Yours truly hadn't won a single round. I came close a couple of times, but, like Dad used to say, "close" only matters in horseshoes and hand grenades. I gave it everything I had, and I still came up short.

When we got back to our rooms for the night, the countdown clock now showed seventy-six hours left. I had a headache, and I was still seeing multicolored spots and flashes in my vision, remnants of looking at virtual alien lasers whizzing at me for seven hours. For the first time, even Malcolm looked tired. He was trying to hide it, but his bloodshot eyes told a different story. And there was no gung-ho talk from him about going to the gym before bed, either. I called Mom.

"I have a surprise for you," she said. "When you come home, Denny wants to throw a party for you at the diner."

"Why?" I asked softly, trying not to sound as beaten as I felt.

"Because we're all so excited to have a science genius around, that's why. Everyone is proud of you."

It wasn't easy to hear that. I missed her, but I also dreaded the possibility of actually going home early. I found myself getting angry at Merlin for getting my hopes up that I could be a hero in the first place.

"Sounds great, Mom. Listen, I gotta go. I love you," I said quickly, then hung up. I sat there on my bed for a quiet moment, then noticed Malcolm watching me. When I looked at him, his glance quickly shifted, and he continued polishing his grandfather's medal.

Kwan had his ear up to the wall again, trying to hear into Ivy and Darla's room.

"Anything interesting going on over there?" I asked him. I wondered if Ivy preferred having an honest-to-goodness room over a sleeping bag in the gloom of the ceiling.

"Nah. Can't hear a thing, anyway." Kwan threw himself on his bed. "I sure hope they fix the damage you did, Earnhardt. I wanna fly actual ships again. I need the *rush*, man." He yawned. "I just hope you guys are ready to get your butts kicked tomorrow. No way I'm going to be the loser who gets sent—"

He cut himself short when our eyes met. As much as he had given me a hard time so far, something in his eyes showed pity for me, and it hurt much more than his wisecracks.

A knock on the door ended the awkward silence.

"Who is it?" Malcolm asked.

"Merlin."

Everyone immediately looked to me. Was he here to take me home already? I went to the door, step by step, like I was making my final trek down death row. When I opened the door, it was Merlin, all right. Alone.

"Good evening." Merlin looked past me. "All of you. Good work today. You should be proud of yourselves. Can I speak with you, Benjamin?" he asked, nodding his head toward the hall.

I wasn't sure what to feel. Would this be the last time I saw the knights? What about Darla? And . . . Ivy? Would I at least get a chance to say good-bye?

"Should I bring my stuff with me now?" I asked Merlin. He squinted in confusion for a moment, then seemed to realize I thought I was going home. He shook his head.

"No. Just bring you."

Merlin and I walked in silence. He took me through a part of HQ I hadn't seen before. We took an elevator up, and when it stopped, it opened on a steel door. Merlin pressed his hand against a scanner by the door. It glowed green as the door unlocked.

"After you," he urged, pointing up a set of stairs.

When I got to the top of them, the sight took my breath away.

31

STEPPING INTO MERLIN'S LAB was like stepping into another world. It was at the very top of HQ, and there was a large opening that allowed a view of the night sky, with an enormous telescope to bring the stars even closer.

There were several easels displaying hand-drawn star constellations with numbers and measurements scrawled everywhere. I ran a hand over the nearest table. The ancient wood was smooth, but I could still feel ridges and pockmarks. I had a feeling this stuff had been in Merlin's possession for hundreds of years.

"I've never shared Percival's fondness for steel," he said as he watched me take it all in.

He ran a hand down the side of a wooden bookcase, touching it so gently that I might have mistaken it for something alive.

"Steel is too cold. It gives nothing back. But wood *breathes*; it holds memories. The blood, sweat, and tears of those it serves. You can feel them in the grain."

I moved tentatively toward to the telescope.

"Go ahead," he nodded.

I stepped onto a wooden stool behind it and pressed my eye to the lens. The view made the stars look like they were at the tip of my nose, like I could reach through the lens and grab them. I remembered a camping trip Dad and I took a few weeks before he died. It was the first time we'd gone together, because it had always been so difficult for him to get weekends off. I could almost hear the crackling campfire and feel Dad's arm around me again. I had never felt safer.

"What do the stars tell you?" Merlin asked. I turned to him, not sure what he meant.

"Maybe it's easier if I explain what they tell *me*. You see, even though there is no true magic—not in the *supernatural* sense—the stars come closest to offering us answers, if we know what questions to ask."

I stepped down from the telescope. "What do you mean?"

"You, Benjamin. The stars have pointed me to *you*."

"But I'm not good at this," I croaked. "I keep losing, and I almost killed everybody and . . . the barfing. Remember the barfing?" I stared at the floor.

He nodded casually. "Hard to forget the barfing," he chuckled. "But Arthur often battled nerves too. Believe it or not."

Arthur. As in *King* Arthur.

Merlin patted my arm. "I have faith that your . . . *mishaps* were merely your nerves getting the better of you. As you and your peers might say—no biggie."

"Wait, Arthur really got nervous?"

"Indeed. Why do you think he was so motivated to create the fantastic legends surrounding himself? Because he was hiding behind them." A bittersweet smile played at the edges of Merlin's lips as he remembered the good old days. He seemed very fond of Arthur. "Later on, of course, he came into his own and didn't need the legends. He had earned his mythic status. Although I'm not sure he ever entirely conquered those butterflies of his."

I looked back at the telescope again. Could the very stars that had been in the night sky every night of my life, the same stars that had twinkled over my one and only camping trip with Dad, be spelling out my destiny? It seemed beyond insane.

"What about Malcolm or Ivy, or any of the other kids?" I asked.

"The stars don't speak of them to me, Benjamin," he countered, unfazed. "They all have their place—there are no accidents in the grand design. But you are meant for greatness."

On the other side of the lab, he handed me something that looked like an X-ray. It showed a cross section of a spaceship that I recognized all too well.

I peered over the familiar curved lines. "This is X-Calibur, isn't it?"

"Yes. But take special notice of the ship's inner structure." He jabbed an area in the center of the image.

I squinted in the soft light for a better look. The image showed that every inch of X-Calibur's body was crammed full of something that looked like thin rods—thousands and thousands of them, folded over and over and crossed and intertwined.

"What is all that in there?" I asked.

"The simple answer? I haven't the foggiest idea. Nobody does. But Percival still had his techs duplicate every *inch* of that maddening structure in the X-Calibur prototypes. Why do you think it's taken *years* to build each of our ships?"

Merlin took the cross section from me and pointed to the alien ship's insides again. "They *change*. We've had other children and teenagers take that pilot seat over the last six years, mostly for testing purposes. But the ship's functions proved to be different for everyone, sometimes even changing *day to day*. I daresay that vessel refuses to be tamed."

"What happened to these other children?" I wondered.

"Most have stayed with us," Merlin explained. "Engineers, techs. The younger ones, mostly. I often lose sleep over the valuable years they've sacrificed for us, believe me."

I thought of Arlo, asleep on his keyboard.

Merlin motioned to the cross section again. "My point, Benjamin, is that what you see on paper is not always the best indicator of success or failure. There's no denying that Malcolm is a highly driven and exceptional child who comes from a legacy of war heroes. But what of *your* legacy? Your father was a hero, too. He died saving lives. Was his heroism any less noble because it took place in a small town that might seem inconsequential to some?"

I shook my head. "No, sir. Not at all."

Merlin nodded and put his hands on my shoulders. "Do you regret helping Darla? You wouldn't be in this predicament of fighting for a spot here if you had allowed her to quit."

I was shocked that Merlin knew about what I'd done for her, but when I remembered the gratitude on Darla's face, my answer was crystal clear.

"No. I would do it again," I said firmly.

"Of course. But can you say the same for Malcolm? Would *he* have put himself on the line for her? Or would he have reveled in the chance to watch a competitor go home?"

I envisioned Malcolm sitting on the edge of his bed, polishing his grandfather's medal. "I'm not sure," I said softly.

Merlin nodded. He seemed fond of that answer, too.

"Being a hero isn't always about strength or courage. Those things eventually come to those who truly have what it takes *in here*." He pointed a finger to my chest. "Compassion cannot be measured or taught, Ben. I still believe you belong here more than anyone."

He finally called me Ben.

"So I'm not going home yet?" I dared to ask.

"No. You're not. And *yet* implies that you going home is a foregone conclusion. That said, your opportunities to impress us are dwindling fast."

Opportunities to impress *us*. So Merlin's faith in me was not limitless. I had to impress *him* sooner or later.

I nodded. "Understood. And thank you."

32

074:53:06

WHEN I GOT BACK to the room, the lights were off and the others had gone to sleep. I slipped into bed and stared up at the countdown clock, wishing Ivy would call again.

I looked over at Malcolm, lying on his side, his back to me. In my heart, I didn't think he was all that different from Tyler or Kwan or Ivy. Their parents were trying to make them be what *they* wanted them to be. Pellinore wanted Ivy to avoid danger at all costs, Kwan's parents wanted him to quit something he loved, and Tyler's parents wanted him to be a kid who'd already reached his potential. If I had to bet money on it, I'd say the medal Malcolm carried around with him was a burden more than anything else, a reminder of a legacy he had no choice in.

Malcolm stirred and turned over to look at me, his face

hard to read in the darkness. "What did Merlin want with you?"

"Oh, just . . . a pep talk. I guess he figured I needed it," I muttered.

There was a moment of silence. "Can I ask you something, Ben?" he whispered. "If we succeed in defending Earth, do you think people will find out about it? Do you think it'll be in books, just like King Arthur and Percival Pellinore?"

"I'm not sure." It was the only answer I had. "But hey— no matter what happens, you're already a hero for saving everyone in the hangar. Thanks again for that. I owe you."

He shifted forward just enough for the light of the window to catch his face. He smiled, but I thought his eyes looked sad.

"Good night, Ben." He retreated into the shadows of his bed.

33

065:14:57

THE HANGAR WALL looked good as new. About two dozen techs still stood guard around the hangar's perimeter. A few of them glared at me.

"Knights, this is it," Pellinore boomed. "Today's training will be longer than yesterday's training in the BSR. Your time in the pods honed your firing, but today is all about flying. Later, *five* of you will finally be given a chance to pilot X-Calibur.

"One of you, however, will be sent home," he continued. "Or, if you'd prefer, stay on and aid us from the ground."

This was my final chance.

"Ben and Darla—you'll race first," Pellinore announced.

Darla was easily ahead of me already after her BSR performance. If I was going to turn this around, I'd have to

190

find a way to beat her. Badly. I'll admit, taking the helmet back from her crossed my mind.

Pellinore gestured to two prototypes parked in the center of the hangar. "Your ships await."

"Rock and roll, Earnhardt. Kick her butt!" Kwan called. I guess there were no hard feelings between us—or at least he liked me better than Darla.

"Good luck," Ivy added. "To both of you."

I strapped myself into my pilot seat. The hangar darkened, and the glowing pyramid-shaped course markers descended from the ceiling.

"Three . . . two . . . one . . . begin!" Pellinore shouted, and we both rocketed into the underground course, flying neck and neck. My heart pounded as we roared around the first curve and onto a straightaway. Darla came around the curve on the outside; I could see her to my right, keeping level with me. I remembered Barrington growling about making use of vertical airspace, so as we soared into the next turn, I pushed forward on my steering controls and dipped down, cutting down the distance I had to travel. My ship tilted until it was almost on its side, but I kept control and grabbed the lead.

My adrenaline was off the charts—I might actually win!
Beep. Beep-beep.

My countdown watch. I dared to look down at it, fearing the worst. Had we lost more time? How much? One of the numbers had bizarrely been replaced by a dollar sign.

I shook my wrist a few times. "Is anybody else seeing this?"

"Seeing what, Ben?" Pellinore replied.

WHOOOSHHH!!!! Darla soared past me. The watch now read **0X4:*X:0%.**

"I think there's something wrong with my—" I began, but the watch suddenly corrected itself. Had I imagined it?

"Something wrong?" Pellinore pressed, but before I could answer, his voice blared through my earpiece again. "Well, that should do it. Excellent flying, Darla. Come back down."

My face fell. Darla had beaten me.

"That was close," Darla offered as we exited our proto-types. "You did really well." She said nothing about her countdown watch flashing random symbols.

I mustered a small smile. "Thanks, but you did better. Congratulations."

She hesitated a moment, then suddenly came at me, arms open, and hugged me. "Thank you, Ben. Thank you so much. For everything." She was already saying good-bye.

As Darla and I walked over to the others, I considered telling them about my countdown watch debacle, but decided against it. Without proof, it would seem like I was just making excuses for the loss.

Pellinore was consulting a clipboard given to him by Barrington. "Next race: Ivy and Kwan."

Merlin, who had crept over to me and was watching everything, whispered, "Don't fret, Benjamin. There'll be plenty more races."

I nodded. "Sure."

And he was right. There *were* dozens of them over the next six hours, but the results were practically a carbon copy of the day before. Malcolm beat everyone he raced against, except when he raced Ivy, and the others also proved their piloting skills. But even though my countdown watch didn't act up again, I only beat Ivy and Darla once—and I'm pretty sure they had conspired to let me win so I didn't look entirely pathetic.

When the day had ended, we all gathered by the hangar door, and Pellinore gave Merlin an expectant glance. Merlin sighed and held out a hand to Pellinore: *I can't. You do it.*

I swallowed as Pellinore clasped a hand on my shoulder, his grip impossibly strong.

"Ben Stone, you are hereby relieved of your duties as a knight. There is but one decision for you to make now. You may leave, or you stay as a grounded member of the RTR."

I felt like I had a million eyes on me. I didn't dare look at the other knights, but I did glance in Merlin's direction. He had his head lowered, eyes shielded. My heart sank.

"I think . . . I'll go home," I answered, but it wasn't easy.

Pellinore nodded. "Very well. Merlin will escort you. I only ask that you respect our code of secrecy."

I hesitated a moment, but only because I was trying

to make sure my voice wouldn't crack too much when I spoke.

"Of course," I managed.

Pellinore looked directly into my eyes. "I wish you well, Ben Stone."

"Thanks for the opportunity," I told him, then found enough courage to give everyone else a wave. "Kick butt when the aliens come, okay?"

Malcolm stood tall, gave me a crisp "Affirmative," and smiled a little bit. It was a smile that said he had come to realize I wasn't all that bad, and that maybe, in some other life, we could have been friends.

"Keep on drivin', Earnhardt," Kwan said with a grin.

I couldn't help but laugh a little. "I don't drive."

His grin only got bigger. "Whatever."

"See ya, Ben," Tyler offered.

Right before I turned away, Darla once again mouthed "Thank you," and Ivy and I exchanged one last glance. Her face looked exactly how I felt inside: confused, conflicted, sad, scared. I couldn't help feeling like our lives had been changed somehow by meeting each other, even if I wasn't exactly sure how yet.

She took a deep breath, then turned away, so I did too.

"C'mon, Merlin," I said softly. "Take me home."

34

059:01:03

MERLIN SAT on Malcolm's bed as I packed my few belongings into Dad's fire-department duffel bag. I had already changed back into the regular clothes I was wearing when I arrived.

"I'm sorry about this, Merlin," I said without looking at him.

"Don't be."

"All that star stuff is . . . well . . . maybe you read it wrong. No offense."

He shot me a concerned glance and handed me my jacket. "None taken. Are you sure you don't want to stay?"

I nodded. "I don't belong here." I picked up the duffel bag and stood in the center of the room. It was hard to believe I was leaving. I took a deep breath. "Let's get outta here." I reached out so he could take my hand and whisk me back to Texas.

"Wait. What about this?" I still had a countdown watch installed on my wrist.

Merlin sighed. "Curses. We can't have you walking around with that on. We'll tell Percival. He can have it taken off right away."

Five minutes later, Merlin and I stepped into the gym. Nobody saw us at first because they were so busy working out against the spar-bots. Pellinore was walking among the knights, offering advice and encouragement as they each battled an opponent.

"Keep it up, knights! You've got to take everything your opponent does into account!" He weaved between the matches effortlessly. "A battle is a battle, whether against a spar-bot or a fleet of alien ships. Don't give up, Tyler! Use your brawn to overpower him! Fantastic, Malcolm— nice advance! You too, Kwan! Parry! Parry! Darla, use your small size to frustrate him!"

Not a word to Ivy.

Merlin held up a hand. "Percival?"

When Pellinore looked over, he was plainly shocked to see me. He pulled a remote out of his pocket and froze the spar-bots in place.

"Benjamin can't leave yet."

"Why not?" Pellinore asked impatiently.

Merlin simply lifted my wrist to reveal my watch. Pellinore sighed and snapped his fingers to a couple of techs who were watching from the corner. They dutifully rushed to get whatever they needed.

"We'll have that off of you in no—" But he didn't get to finish the sentence. Everything happened in a flash.

"Look out!" Ivy screamed as, with a *THWUNK*, Pellinore was nearly knocked unconscious. Behind him, a spar-bot held its sword high. *"Win! Win! Win!"* it repeated, its voice changing pitch and speed like an old cassette player munching on a tape. Its eyes flickered on and off like mini strobe lights, clearly malfunctioning.

Pellinore's eyes rolled up in his head as he went to his knees and wobbled. Darla screamed, and Kwan and Tyler yelped in surprise. If that sword had been real, it would have sliced Pellinore's head in half.

THWACK-THWACK-THWACK! Malcolm lunged at the spar-bot, pummeling it with sword strikes, but it whirled and effortlessly knocked the sword out of his hand. It grabbed Malcolm by his jumpsuit and tossed him like he was a half-empty bag of potato chips. Tyler managed to catch him, but the two toppled backward.

"Get away, knights!" Merlin shouted, waving his arms in a panic as he pushed Darla and Kwan aside.

Pellinore was just getting to his feet when the spar-bot went for him again and grabbed him in a one-armed choke hold from behind. Pellinore kicked and flailed, gasping for air. He threw a few backward elbows into the spar-bot's chest.

Ivy screamed and rushed the spar-bot when it grabbed

her father. She tried smacking it with her sword, causing it to throw aside its own weapon and grab Ivy's neck as well, lifting her off the floor.

"*En garde!*"

I stood on the other side of the gym, holding a practice sword, crouched in a fighting stance. The crazed spar-bot turned to look at me, its eyes clicking and blinking.

"Benjamin, don't!" Merlin cried, but I ignored him.

"Are you deaf?! I said *en garde*, you overgrown toaster!" I yelled at the spar-bot.

Thankfully, the spar-bot's programmed response to *en garde* remained intact, and it dropped both Ivy and Pellinore to engage me in a fight. It swooped up its sword, yanked a second one from the fist of a frozen spar-bot nearby, and charged at me, wildly swinging both like a psychotic spar-bot zombie ninja.

WHOOSH!! It tried to slice me in half vertically, from head to floor. I dodged the first swing, and then another. Both swords hit the floor hard and their protective casings shattered, exposing the sharp tips underneath. I spun away, once, then twice, *fast,* barely avoiding the blades as they sliced past me and tore through the padded walls.

I backed up alongside the wall, eyes never leaving the spar-bot. When I got to another wall and had nowhere to go, I fought back, my one plastic sword whacking against the spar-bot's two metal-tipped ones. We traded dozens of swings in mere seconds—parry, parry, lunge, fleche, lunge, neither of us making contact with anything but each other's swords, everything moving fast and furious. When I noticed that the tip of my sword had been cracked by the many blows, I had an idea.

I spun sideways again, and with two hands on my sword, I smashed it down on the ground as hard as I could. It worked. The entire plastic casing broke away to expose the metal underneath. The spar-bot lunged for me, and I ducked and drove my sword upward through the spar-bot's torso. The tip found a seam between two of its metal panels and the sword continued all the way out of its back. It fell to the floor with a lifeless clang.

"You lose," I breathed, catching my breath, every nerve in my body zinging.

The gym door opened, and the two techs hurried in with a countdown watch machine.

"Sorry for the delay, sir. We're ready to remove the . . ." The tech trailed off, eyes wide at the sight of Pellinore on his knees, still trying to collect himself, while a very worried Ivy stood by his side.

I looked to the faces of the other knights. I had honestly forgotten that anyone else was even in the room while I was fighting; all else had been blocked from my mind. Kwan, Darla, and Tyler gaped at me, and Malcolm looked utterly baffled. And Merlin? A smile played on his lips, like he'd just seen the greatest magic trick in the world.

The two techs rushed over to assist Ivy in helping her father to his feet. There was only silence until he flapped a hand at the countdown watch machine.

"Get that out of here," he told the techs. Then he looked from me to Merlin. Merlin gave him a wide-eyed shrug. Across the gym, my duffel bag sat, still packed and ready to go home.

"Change of plans," Pellinore announced, his voice raspy from almost being choked to death. "Nobody's going anywhere yet. You're *all* going to get a chance at X-Calibur tomorrow."

35

"WHERE DID YOU LEARN to fight like that?" Kwan asked after we'd returned to our room.

I shrugged anxiously. All along I had wanted to be special, but now that I had everyone's attention, I didn't want it. Not like this.

"I'd like to see you square off against Pellinore in a swordfight," Tyler whispered in awe.

Me against Percival Pellinore, an original knight of the Round Table? I shook my head, embarrassed. "No way. Not a chance."

Malcolm gave an exasperated snort. "If the aliens want to forgo ships in favor of a swordfight, Ben can fight them all for us," he offered sarcastically.

He eyed me like I couldn't be trusted, like I had tricked everyone. But if anybody had been tricked, it was me.

201

How was I supposed to know I could do that? Malcolm did have a point, though. When it came to flying ships, I was still the least skilled here.

Even after we turned the lights off, I couldn't stop thinking about what had happened.

When lives are on the line, it's all about doing, not thinking, Dad had said. I looked to the window and could barely make out a few stars glimmering through the London fog. The name *Dredmore* popped into my brain uninvited. It wasn't a something, it was a some*one*—I could feel that in my gut—and whatever Dredmore was, he was coming to wreak havoc on my planet. Seeing Pellinore knocked to the floor by a spar-bot of his own design made me wonder what our chances of survival really were.

Suddenly, the countdown clock went blank.

I sat up, heart hammering, waiting. Two words popped up: **ME . . . AGAIN.**

A smile exploded onto my face as three letters flashed: **BSR.**

I stopped outside the BSR and looked up at the ceiling, waiting for the panel to slide open and reveal Ivy. I heard faint sounds of a battle coming from the other side of the BSR doors: alien ships soaring through space and lasers screeching. I squeezed through the opening, and for a moment my gut twisted in nerves.

"Hello?" I shouted over the storm of virtual laser fire around me. There was no answer. As I walked deeper into the vast space, an alien ship surged right at me. A hand suddenly grabbed me by the shirt and yanked me backward, into the open hatch of a pod. With the virtual outer space turned on, the pod had been camouflaged.

I crammed into the pod's lone pilot seat with Ivy.

"I just saved your life," she grinned. "You were about to become space mush. We're even now, okay?"

When I didn't answer, she shrugged. "Okay, maybe not."

"Listen, about the gym—" I began. I wanted to tell her that I hadn't tried to trick anyone, but she cut me off.

"Thank you, Ben. You saved my life *and* my father's. He gets on my nerves sometimes, sure, but . . . I still kinda like having him around," she said with a swallow.

"You're welcome." I took a deep breath. In the tiny pod, she was practically sitting in my lap.

"By the way, Darla told me what you did for her with the helmet. That was brilliant."

"Oh. Thanks." I wondered what else Darla had told her.

"I couldn't sleep, so I figured I'd get in some target practice for tomorrow," Ivy explained, gesturing to the pod's windshield and the virtual battle beyond it.

"Your dad doesn't encourage you like he does the others," I found myself blurting out. "But he loves you a lot. More than anything."

Ivy smiled but changed the subject. "Where did you learn to swordfight? It was incredible."

I groaned. "I don't know, it just happened. An instinct, I guess."

"Well, whatever it was, you've got to channel it again tomorrow," she said determinedly.

She jumped out of the pod and led me through the halls of HQ, into restricted areas I hadn't seen yet.

"I was wondering . . . " I whispered along the way. "I heard that you're the reason we have X-Calibur in the first place. Is that true?"

She seemed surprised. "Who told you that?"

"Let's just say you're not the only one who's good at spying on your father and Merlin," I admitted, and her face lit up.

"Bravo," she said excitedly and gave me a high five. "I'm the reason they were able to get the ship to turn on."

"What do you mean?" I asked.

"When I was eight, I was sneaking around in here and found my way into X-Calibur. I really just wanted to see what my father was doing all the time." Ivy suddenly reached out and pushed me back against the wall, putting a finger to her mouth. I looked down the hall and saw Arlo turning a corner. Luckily, he turned down another hall and out of sight.

Ivy continued walking cautiously and whispering. "X-Calibur was essentially a massive paperweight at that point. Nobody could turn it on. That's why my father had all the techs build imitations of it, because the real one had proven useless."

I turned to her. "But it responded to you?"

"As soon as I touched the steering controls, it powered

up. Everyone was shocked. But I couldn't get it to do anything else. I had no clue what it was even *supposed* to do. I was a kid. They kept telling me to push buttons and panels, but nothing happened."

"That's when they started bringing in more kids?"

"Yes. They found that older kids could get the buttons and things to respond, although not always in the way they wanted."

I remembered Merlin explaining to me that the buttons inside X-Calibur seemed to change daily, like the ship didn't want to be tamed. As Ivy and I turned a corner, we passed an office that had a glass window on its door. I blinked quickly: I could have sworn the countdown clock inside flashed those strange symbols again. But when I blinked again, the numbers there were correct.

I was about to shout ahead to Ivy when I heard a hum to my left. I turned. There was another hallway that branched off this one. The ceiling light at the start of the hallway was getting brighter, then darker, then brighter again, humming with each pulse as the electricity level rose and fell.

The light seemed to be beckoning me. Just like in my dream. I pinched myself.

"Hey, what are you waiting for?" Ivy suddenly asked, startling me. She was headed back this way. Everything returned to normal.

I nodded to the hallway where the light had been pulsing. "What's down there?"

Ivy shrugged. "Lots of things. Satellite monitoring stations, engineering department. It's also another way to get to the hangar."

"Where the ships are?"

"Yeah. Come on," she said, waving. "We're almost there."

I gave the hall one last puzzled look and hurried after Ivy. Less than a minute later, we had reached our destination.

Ivy grinned. "Ready to see something that's not on my father's tour?"

We were standing at the end of the hall, looking at . . . a wall. Ivy pulled out a key chain that had a little digital voice recorder on it. Right before she pressed PLAY, she grabbed my hand.

"Hold on," she cautioned, and our fingers interlocked. *This is the greatest moment of my life,* I thought.

Pellinore's voice came out of the little recorder. He said just one word: "Protector."

I felt the unmistakable magnetic pull of the floor in my feet and legs. Ivy and I dropped as the panel we were standing on plummeted down a steel shaft, taking us with it. The plunge lasted only a split second, but we dropped about ten feet to a secret, shadowy room. The magnetic pull vanished from our legs and we stepped forward.

"What is this?" I squinted, until my eyes adjusted to the darkness.

A clear cylinder of glass, about seven feet tall and four feet wide, stood on a steel base. My eyes widened when I realized there was something floating in it. Ivy reached down to hit a switch at the cylinder's base. A light shone up into the fluid. My jaw dropped.

There was an alien suspended in there. It was dead, partially mummified, about five feet tall and skinny, with greenish gray skin. But the thing that really got to me was its face. It was wrinkled and scrunched together, eyes closed. It looked a little bit like an old man, a creature that might pass for part alien and part human, with an undeniable softness to its face.

"This is the alien scientist that flew X-Calibur to Earth, isn't it?" I asked.

Ivy nodded.

I stepped closer to the glass and put my hand against it, inches from the alien. "You know, Merlin said something to me last night about there being no accidents."

"What do you mean?" Ivy's finger traced the base of the cylinder absentmindedly.

"Just that everything that's meant to happen *does* happen. I think it must have been your dad's destiny to find this alien and X-Calibur, don't you? There's no way it was just blind luck."

Ivy's brow furrowed. "Of course it wasn't blind luck. He and Merlin had been tracking the origin of King Arthur's sword, so it made sense that it led them to the alien."

I turned to her. "Huh?

"Didn't they explain how they found the ship when you were brought into HQ?"

"Your father said it was discovered in his travels, that's all."

Ivy turned and walked deeper into the mysterious room, explaining along the way. "When the ship crashed on Earth, a sliver of its body was ripped off during atmosphere entry. A blacksmith eventually got the metal and forged it into the sword used by King Arthur."

My mind was reeling. "But X-Calibur, the ship, looked flawless. I didn't see any slivers missing," I countered.

"It came off the very bottom. You can see the mark if you know where to look."

We quickened our pace. "How do you know this?" I asked.

"My father has it written down in his files, in case something ever happens to him or Merlin."

Ivy arrived at a wall that had a window of glass built into it, though it was too dark to see inside.

"After Arthur and the other knights passed away, Merlin and my father realized there was something special about Arthur's sword. It was like no metal they'd ever seen. It ultimately led them to the crashed ship."

I pointed to the dark piece of glass in the wall. "So what's in there?"

"See for yourself." She pointed to a switch next to the glass, and as I leaned forward to click it, I felt like everything was moving in slow motion, the world around me melting away, just as it had done while I fought the spar-bot.

There was a massive sword behind the glass, its

razor-sharp blade glistening like water. There was zero doubt about where the metal of that blade had come from.

The sword's handle was adorned with jewels—rubies and emeralds, probably worth millions of dollars. And even though the handle itself looked well-worn, the jewels sparkled with an almost magical brilliance.

"Excalibur," I breathed. *"It's real."*

36

048:51:24

IN THE EARLY HOURS of the next morning, we found ourselves in an abandoned soccer stadium. The place was large enough to hold over fifty thousand people, but now it was in bad shape and long forgotten in the middle of the English countryside. No "civilians," Pellinore assured us, would see us out there.

In the middle of the empty, shadowy field, brightly lit by the glow of its own mechanics, stood X-Calibur.

In the light cast by the spaceship, Pellinore paced before us. "We're going to start things off differently," he explained. He nodded to Merlin, a cue to show us a black velvet bag. "This bag contains six numbered rocks. Grab one, and keep it in your fist until told to reveal them. Understood?"

The six of us nodded. Darla gave me a little smile and whispered, "I'm glad you're still here."

I smiled back. "Me too."

"Today will determine which of you will pilot X-Calibur. The chosen knight will train all day tomorrow with X-Calibur, while four of the remaining will continue working with the prototypes."

Merlin walked down the line, giving each of us a chance to reach into the bag. "Okay. Reveal your numbers."

We opened our fists. Incredibly, Malcolm had picked number one, Ivy had picked number two, Darla had picked three, Kwan four, Tyler five, and me last. If our rock choices were fate at work, then it didn't say much for me.

"Malcolm, you're up," Pellinore said. "Show us what you can do in X-Calibur. Use the stadium airspace any way you see fit. *Dazzle* us."

Malcolm stood at attention. "Yes, sir. And the weapons?"

"Fire at will," Pellinore stated firmly, then added, "To *that* side of the stadium only, please." He pointed across the field to the opposite side of the stadium. Malcolm's brow furrowed, as did mine and everyone else's.

"I'm . . . not sure I follow, sir," he stammered. "You want me to shoot *at the stadium*?"

"Correct. How else will we get a taste of X-Calibur's weaponry? Have no fear; I own this stadium. It's mine to destroy." He gave us all a wink.

"Yes, sir!" Malcolm barked, then hurried across the

field. When he got to the ship, he looked back and gave us all a crisp salute. He'd been waiting his whole life for this moment.

As we waited for the ship to move, Pellinore fidgeted like a father watching his son take his first at-bat in a Little League game. "Talk to me, Malcolm," he said when he couldn't endure the suspense anymore. He nodded, listening to Malcolm respond through the earpiece, and then X-Calibur began to hum again and slowly rise. The fact that Malcolm had gotten the ship to even take off was apparently a big deal.

X-Calibur was only a few feet off the ground, though, when it suddenly swung around, its tail end almost clipping a few techs who quickly jumped out of the way. We gasped as the ship suddenly whipped its back end in the *other* direction, still hovering in place. More techs jumped for cover.

"Malcolm, what's going on?!" Pellinore cried.

I put on my helmet, hoping Malcolm's voice would be audible over the comm system.

"I'm not doing anything, sir!" Malcolm grunted, fighting the controls. "The ship is doing it on its own! I think it's malfunctioning!"

I looked to the other knights, who had all followed my lead and put on their helmets. I didn't think any of us had bargained for this.

"*You're* the pilot!" Pellinore snapped. "That ship is a *machine*! *Make* it work for you! You're a *Gunn*!"

Pellinore's tactic worked. Malcolm got the ship to stop spinning, and it rose straight up with the grace of a bird.

"Excellent, Malcolm," Pellinore said. "Now show us what the ship can do."

The back of X-Calibur lit up even more as Malcolm gave it power. He could fly, there was no doubt about that, but the ship wasn't doing anything all that different from the prototypes. As Malcolm soared around in wide laps, I glanced at Merlin and Pellinore. They had clearly hoped for something more. Something that would give us a fighting chance against Dredmore.

The ship whipped around to face away from us and Malcolm unleashed a barrage of weapon fire. Every blast shot from X-Calibur's talon-shaped wings was like concentrated lightning, and the damage inflicted to the stadium was devastating. Entire sections crumbled as support beams were obliterated.

Pellinore and Merlin squinted as they observed the destruction. So far, X-Calibur had proven to be just another ship. And a temperamental one at that. Would it be enough to protect mankind?

X-Calibur stopped firing, then spun around and went low, cruising about ten feet over the stadium's dead grass.

"Talk to me, Malcolm," Pellinore said. But there was silence.

"Malcolm, you there?"

I yanked off my helmet to watch X-Calibur veer sideways and dip even lower.

"Malcolm?!" Pellinore repeated, but the ship swerved again and circled just a few feet off the ground. *It's looking for a place to land,* I thought.

The second X-Calibur touched down, I heard a tiny beep. I looked to my countdown watch and gulped. It pulsed rapidly: **XXX:XX:XX**. The pulsing sped up—brighter, softer, brighter, softer. I couldn't take my eyes off it.

In the middle of the field, Malcolm exited X-Calibur and jogged toward us, a triumphant grin on his face. Pellinore greeted him. "How did she handle?"

"Brilliantly," Malcolm chirped. "Once I got the ship under control. There was interference on the comm line, though."

With my eyes on my countdown watch and those pulsing "X"s, I thought, *Of course there was interference. It's the same thing that's causing my watch to—*

"Hey, something's wrong with my watch," Darla suddenly cried.

"Mine too!" Tyler confirmed.

I glanced at my own watch again and felt a chill. One by one, the others held out their wrists: **000:00:00**.

The teams were running toward us, muttering into their headpieces.

"What's this about?" Pellinore demanded.

"We just got confirmation from HQ. It's go time!" one of the techs shouted in terror.

"The aliens, sir! *They're already here!*"

37

000:00:00

WE SCRAMBLED to get back to HQ in total chaos. The techs hurried to load X-Calibur into the cargo copter, even though Malcolm practically got down on his knees and pleaded to fly the ship straight from the stadium and into battle.

When we arrived, we hurried into a war room command center. The techs brought up images of six menacing alien ships, two or three times the size of our own, in the skies over a small English town about fifty miles from HQ. Was Dredmore inside one of them? The possibility made me shudder.

Pellinore was livid as he ordered the removal of our watches. I stuck my arm in the metal box and felt a flash of heat near my wrist, then the sound of metal being sheared in two. I eyed the severed watch's now-blank face,

215

remembering all the "X"s that had been there. Had any of the other watches shown "X"s before changing to zeroes? Or just mine? I realized now that those flashing "X"s had been trying to communicate with me for some time now. Had X-Calibur been trying to *warn* me that the aliens were going to be here early?

"They've been using our tracking signal as a directional tool!" a tech shouted, waving a computer printout triumphantly. "It led them straight to us. They must have disrupted the signal to compromise the arrival estimates." He exhaled heavily. "We never accounted for this, sir."

Pellinore was speechless as techs began hijacking every form of communication in the town beneath the aliens: cell phone systems, land lines, television, radio, even emergency systems. We had to keep this battle, and the aliens, as secret as possible.

"Any damage so far?" Pellinore asked, but the techs shook their heads. The sky had grown increasingly gray and cloudy, helping to make the aliens less visible.

"Initiate fog cover!" Barrington growled.

Tiny missiles full of concentrated chemicals launched from the roof of HQ. When they detonated within the clouds, the town was shrouded in an even thicker layer of fog. Unless the aliens infiltrated to street level, it would be difficult for anyone on the ground to see what was about to go on above them.

"Benjamin, listen." Beside me, Merlin leaned in close.

"I'll never persuade Percival to let you pilot X-Calibur. But you *will* fly a prototype."

What? I hadn't seen that coming. "The techs finished another ship?"

He hesitated, and I got a feeling I wasn't going to like his answer. "No. You're going to take Ivy's place. Percival's decision, not mine."

"No way," I said firmly. "I want to do my part, Merlin. Believe me, I do. But I'm not replacing Ivy. She deserves this chance."

A hand suddenly rested on my shoulder, and I turned, startled to see Pellinore standing behind me. "He won't go up," Merlin said.

Pellinore's face contorted as Ivy approached.

"What's going on?" she asked, standing next to her father with her arms crossed. Merlin and Pellinore froze.

"Your father was just telling me I'm not going to be able to fly," I explained. I looked up at Pellinore, eyes narrowed. "Right, sir?"

Pellinore looked pained. "Yes. Congratulations, Ivy." He gave her a hug like it might be the last time he'd ever see her. When he released her, Ivy quickly wiped a tear from her eye and gave me a smile.

"Are the ships ready?" Pellinore asked, composed again. "And the pilot uniforms?"

Right on cue, Arlo rolled in a rack holding six new pilot jumpsuits, each constructed of millions of thread-thin

217

steel fibers laced together, like stretchable armor. Malcolm, Kwan, Tyler, Ivy, and Darla eagerly grabbed their new uniforms and shiny steel helmets, leaving mine hanging alone.

I rushed over to Darla before she could leave to change. "The helmet," I whispered. "If you give me the old one, I'll take out the scenery rig and install it in this new one—"

She cut me off with a shake of her head. "Ben, I don't need it anymore. All those hours of prototype races yesterday? Halfway through, I took my helmet off, and guess what? I was fine! You helped me more than you could have even imagined."

"I'm glad," I said, and I meant it. She grabbed my hand. "Come downstairs and see us off!"

I grinned. "Wouldn't miss it for the world."

X-Calibur was parked next to the four prototypes, ready for action. Merlin had come with us, but Pellinore had stayed upstairs in the war room. I think he couldn't deal with watching Ivy leave for battle. I couldn't blame him.

Malcolm, Kwan, Tyler, and Darla headed toward their ships, but Ivy paused beside me. I gave Merlin a sideways glare, and he sheepishly turned and walked a few feet away.

"You'll do amazing up there," I told Ivy. "I've got a front row seat for watching you kick alien butt."

She suddenly pulled me into a fierce hug. I noticed Merlin looking over his shoulder, watching us. He quickly looked away again.

"I know my father wasn't going to let me do this," Ivy

whispered in my ear. "Thank you for sticking up for me. You never stop . . . being you, do you?"

I shrugged. "I'm the only me I have."

She ran off to her ship and gave a final wave. Merlin returned to my side and joined me in waving back. "God-speed, knights!"

X-Calibur and the four prototypes fired up, and an entire wall of the hangar slid up to reveal an underground runway.

"They'll exit undetected on the city outskirts," Merlin explained.

If all went according to plan, the rest of the world would have no knowledge of what was about to occur: the first battle between aliens and humans. As the ships soared into the tunnel and out of sight, I realized I cared about the knights as much as I'd ever cared about anyone. They had become my friends. My stomach was in knots. Would I ever see them again?

38

THE WAR ROOM was crammed wall to wall with every single member of the RTR. Every set of eyes was glued to five large screens that showed our knights rocketing through the sky, ready to engage the enemy. Each knight had a personal screen with their name at the bottom, and their voices came over the war room's speaker system.

"Talk to me, knights," Pellinore barked. He had rolled up his sleeves, raring to go. He'd been waiting hundreds of years for this.

"I got one in my sights!" Kwan's shaky voice exploded over the speakers. Before Pellinore could respond, we all watched as Kwan fired.

I looked to Malcolm's screen, wondering why he hadn't fired yet. It showed nothing but gray sky.

"Where's Malcolm?" I wondered. A split second later,

everyone in the sky was firing, aliens and knights alike. The battle had begun. There was so much happening on the screens that it was difficult to keep up.

"I got one!" Ivy crowed. One of the screens zoomed in on an alien ship that had just been damaged, its front end smoking and charred. Everyone in the room cheered.

"Great work, Ivy. But be careful!" Pellinore growled. "And where *is* Malcolm?!"

"We've got him now!" a tech yelled, and we whipped our gazes to Malcolm's screen. For some reason the ship was flying straight up, *away* from the action.

"What's he doing?!" Pellinore roared.

Still no answer.

"I hit one!" Tyler suddenly shouted. There was the sound of an explosion, and both Darla and Ivy also shouted that they'd scored hits. Our screens showed damage on *four* of the six alien ships, and none of our knights had even been hit once. They really were kicking butt up there!

There were more cheers, but Pellinore, Merlin, and I were focused on X-Calibur as it continued to climb higher.

"Malcolm, do you have control of your ship?" Pellinore demanded. "If you can hear me, I expect an answer!"

"It's me," Malcolm finally answered. "Trust me, sir. I have a plan."

I exchanged a confused glance with Merlin as X-Calibur hung in midair for a moment, at least a mile above the others. The front end of the ship dipped down as if in slow motion and then took off, plunging into a nosedive.

Malcolm let loose a barrage of weapon fire, and a storm of lasers rained down from X-Calibur's talon wings. Several of the shots connected with the four previously hit alien ships, and two of them, already paralyzed by their damage, exploded.

Our screens were clouded by views of smoke and alien debris. The only ship of ours that I could still make out up there was Tyler's. Another alien ship came into view, with pieces of its battered outer casing flapping in the wind. With the casing loose, we saw the meat of the ship: two separate modules, with a thinner point in the middle. Within the smoke and flames roaring out of that middle section were flashes of energy—the nucleus of the ship's power.

Barrington lit up and moved closer to the screen. "*Now* we're talking!" he growled.

Tyler fired at the ship's middle section, and it was obliterated into virtually nothing.

"YESSS!" Tyler shouted triumphantly, and Barrington pumped his fist so hard that he knocked over a hapless tech.

But the celebration was short-lived.

"I think I'm in trouble," Malcolm muttered over the speakers. We all looked to X-Calibur's screen. He *was* in trouble: The two remaining alien ships were on his tail, bearing down on him. Malcolm kept trying to whip X-Calibur around to face them or find a way to rotate his weapons in their direction, but he couldn't pull it off. The aliens closed in like wolves.

We watched and waited. The second those aliens

decided to fire, he would be toast, *unless* he found a way to make X-Calibur do something extraordinary. Malcolm Gunn was about to give up his life, and no history book would remember him.

I winced as a series of weapon blasts rocked the sky. I squeezed my eyes shut at the sound of the massive explosion that came next.

Suddenly, everyone in the war room cheered louder than ever. I opened my eyes. Ivy and Darla had come to Malcolm's rescue. The aliens, so focused on chasing X-Calibur, hadn't seen the two girls sneak up behind them. While Ivy and Darla unloaded all they had into the alien ships, Kwan and Tyler finished off the damaged ones. More explosions lit up the sky, and just like that, it was over. The Round Table Reboot had successfully protected Earth from alien invaders.

39

PELLINORE SPARED no expense for the celebration in the atrium of HQ. I was wearing a suit that he had given me for the occasion, only the second time in my life that I'd worn one. Ivy was wearing a green dress that made her eyes even more radiant. She and the other knights beamed with a sense of fulfillment that I wished I could have shared. I felt like I was crashing somebody else's party.

Malcolm strolled around the room in his own new suit and tie. Techs congratulated him and shook his hand while Pellinore walked by his side. Tyler strolled over to me, chowing down on a massive plate of rice and grilled vegetables.

"You gotta try the brussels sprouts," he said through a mouthful. "They rock."

I wrinkled my nose. "No thanks. But hey—awesome job up there. I saw you using moves from Barrington's class. Genius!"

He grinned. "Thanks. Maybe I'm smart enough for college after all, huh?"

"Definitely," I replied.

When Ivy saw Tyler and me talking, she came over and gave me a playful nudge. "Look at you. All *fancy*."

I tried not to blush as Kwan and Darla joined us. We'd all developed a bond, especially now that the competition was over. Even Kwan and Darla seemed to be enjoying each other's company.

"How awesome are we?" Kwan crowed happily and offered us burgers from his plate. We each grabbed one and tapped them together with one of Tyler's brussels sprouts like glasses of champagne. Still, I couldn't help feeling like an outsider. *They* had been up in the sky fighting, not me.

"The aliens never even had a chance against us," Tyler boasted, and it was true. The aliens had been way outmatched.

"Kinda sucks that the world doesn't know how lucky it is to have us, huh?" Tyler sighed.

"All I know is, there's no *way* I'm going to quit surfing now," Kwan said.

"What about your parents?" I wondered.

"They'll just have to deal. I'll still do my best at school, but you know what? I'm an *action* guy. And the world already has plenty of doctors and lawyers."

"I'll toast to that," Darla said with a grin. She and Kwan bumped bacon cheeseburgers again. The rest of us laughed as Malcolm came over to join us.

"Hey. I just wanted to thank you, Ivy," he said softly. "And you too, Darla. If you both hadn't helped me up there . . . I wouldn't be here right now. I wouldn't be *anywhere*."

Ivy waved him off. "We're all on the same team here, remember?"

"I second that," Darla added.

"Then I want to apologize," he countered. "To all of you. I've been kind of an idiot. I got so caught up in trying to be who I'm supposed to be, and the truth is, I forgot we were a team. But from now, I'll remember. That's a promise."

He reached into his pocket and pulled out his grandfather's war medal, eyeing it with a new sense of peace. "I'm going to give this back to my grandfather as soon as I get home. This was *his* life, not mine." He looked at me after saying that, and I gave him a little nod.

"Can I have everyone's attention please?" Pellinore announced into a microphone. He was standing on a stage by the atrium's back wall. "Today is a day of celebration. A victory for each and every one of us."

Everyone applauded.

"But that victory is especially sweet for our courageous

knights." The cheers grew as everyone turned to look our way. "Let's hear a speech from our heroes! Where's our esteemed X-Calibur pilot?" Pellinore boomed.

Malcolm was making his way to the stage when there was a sudden deep rumble. A moment later it came again, and this time the walls around us shook. My insides went numb with horror. Merlin and I exchanged a glance, and that's when I knew.

Dredmore.

There was a cracking sound above us as half the ceiling gave way under the force of some kind of blast. Chunks of concrete and metal suddenly rained down as we scattered like ants. The bulk of the destruction had occurred above the stage, and I got a fleeting glimpse of Malcolm and Pellinore getting hit and falling, unconscious. I grabbed Ivy as Kwan grabbed Darla and Tyler tried to grab *all* of us, doing his best to shield us as we scrambled aside.

The floor was already littered with people who had been hit. For the rest of us, it was chaos. When I dared to look up, I wished I hadn't. Through the massive hole in the ceiling I saw various ravaged levels of HQ, all the way up to a glimpse of the dusky sky high above. Through the smoke and dust, I could see alien ships up there. *Tons* of them.

It had all been a ruse. They'd lulled us into a false sense of security, letting us believe five *kids* had saved mankind. We were sitting ducks, and the planet was clueless to the threat because *we had kept everything a secret.*

Someone grabbed me from behind. I whirled to see Merlin. He wobbled slightly as a trickle of blood ran down his forehead. I grabbed him, held him up. "This is it, Benjamin," he whispered urgently.

"This is what?" I pleaded. Over his shoulder I saw frenzied techs dragging Malcolm and Pellinore, both out cold, to safety. Merlin seized my face and looked me square in the eye.

"Become your destiny."

40

I RAN THROUGH the crumbling halls of HQ with Ivy, Kwan, Darla, and Tyler. Entire sections of the walls and the floors fell away around us, forcing us to change direction and take new paths.

"Where are we going?!" Kwan panicked as he dodged a piece of flying debris.

"We've gotta get up there and fight!" I shouted. If we could get to our equipment and weapons in time, we'd still stand a fighting chance. "We'll need our helmets, then we'll get into our ships!"

I led the way down another corridor as the ground shook beneath our feet. The lights above us flickered and sparked, and we had to brace ourselves against each other as we ran just to keep our balance.

"Who's going to fly X-Calibur?" Darla asked.

"*I am*," I told her without hesitation.

Up ahead, I spotted something moving down the hallway. I almost mistook them for hefty, oversized humans at first, but one of them wasn't wearing a helmet, and when it looked our way, I heard Kwan let out a small cry of surprise. Its eyes were two long slits, and its nose was a shortened hook. A large mouth stretched around its head, all the way under its ears, full of hundreds of tiny, jagged teeth, and a row of fleshy spikes ran across the top of its head.

The creature hissed, and then he and his crew turned and came rushing toward us with metal clubs, the tips sizzling like cattle prods.

"This could be a problem," Kwan whispered.

"C'mon!" I grabbed Ivy's hand as we all turned and ran. How on earth were we going to get out of this?

Another blast practically knocked us over, but we stayed close, using each other as support. Tyler pulled Darla up as she tripped on a cracked floor panel. I stole a glance behind me and saw the aliens struggling through falling debris.

"Uh, guys?" Kwan pointed to the ceiling. "There's more coming from up there, too."

A handful of them were climbing down from a hole in the ceiling, like termites crawling out of the woodwork. I felt Ivy's hand squeeze mine tighter. This didn't look good.

Suddenly, a wall crumbled up ahead and then collapsed, giving us a view into another hallway. "That way!"

We climbed through the wall and down the hall, but we didn't get far. The floor had collapsed into the level beneath it. When I saw what was down there, I was flooded with new adrenaline.

It was Pellinore's secret room.

"We gotta get outta here!" Kwan shrieked, the aliens getting closer with every second. But there was no place else to run now, and we had backed ourselves into a corner at the end of this hall.

"Stay here!" I shouted, but Ivy grabbed me by the shoulders. "Trust me," I breathed, before she could say anything.

The hallway floor had collapsed at an angle, with one side of it still intact. I got down on my butt and slid down the fallen floor, entering the secret room and rushing to the glass display case in the wall, the one that held Excalibur. The glass already had a crack running down the center of it, but it was still intact and strong, six inches thick. I could see a vague reflection of myself in the glass. I smirked at the ridiculousness of me wearing a suit and tie right now, then grabbed a chunk of broken concrete and smashed it against the glass until it shattered around me. As I grabbed the legendary sword, I was overcome by memories of Dad at my bedside, whispering to me the stories about King Arthur and Excalibur. In that moment I felt the closest I'd felt to Dad since his death.

I heard Darla scream above me, so I whirled and scurried up the fallen hallway, taking the heavy sword with me. Back in the hallway, a dozen aliens were ready to pounce on my fellow knights. Tyler didn't waste any time in unleashing a guttural battle cry and charging the nearest alien. It was so taken aback that Tyler managed to grab it around the belly and send it flying backward into its peers, who toppled like bowling pins. That was all I needed to rush forward and raise my sword.

"Hey! Butt-uglies!" I yelled, and the aliens turned, scrambling to get up. A few charged at me, and, with both hands around the handle of Excalibur, I went to work. *Doing, not thinking.* The crazy thing is that the weight of Excalibur made *me* feel bigger and stronger, like I'd been wielding a sword my whole life.

I had already taken out half the aliens by the time Tyler finally got his wrestling opponent to pass out. As he scrambled out from under the unconscious creature, Ivy rushed over and grabbed the cattle prod thingy the alien had dropped. Then she turned and rammed it into the back of another alien I was fighting. The creature shuddered and shook, its eyes lighting up blue. There was a horrific odor, like something rotten being cooked over an open fire, then the alien toppled forward, fried from the inside out.

Darla and Kwan took Ivy's lead and seized two more of the fallen weapons from the aliens I had already defeated. We worked like a team, and the floor was soon littered with aliens we'd defeated.

But we still had plenty to do. The hallways were hardly

distinguishable anymore, just crumbled walls and floors and ceilings everywhere. It could take all day to find our way out.

"Which way do we go?" Ivy asked. "Any idea?"

Then I saw it: a lone ceiling light that had remained intact about fifty feet away. It was pulsing. I looked twenty feet past it and saw another one, also pulsing, beckoning me forward.

I sighed with relief. All the others looked down the hall, confused.

"What is it?" Ivy asked.

"X-Calibur."

41

AS X-CALIBUR'S virtual seat belt strapped me in with Excalibur at my side, I could still hear the walls of the underground hangar rumbling around me. I was pretty sure that all of HQ would be nothing more than a cavern of dust in a few minutes.

Ivy, Darla, Kwan, and Tyler had rushed to their own ships without a single word or glance. No good lucks, or hugs, or anything else—there was no time for good-byes.

The hangar wall in front of us slid up and revealed the underground runway. I gripped X-Calibur's steering mechanism and took a shaky breath as I lifted off. So far, the ship didn't feel all that different from a prototype.

The others hovered in place, waiting for me to take the lead.

"Let's do this," I commanded, and blasted into the tunnel. Within seconds, it sloped steeply upward, and then daylight appeared like a lightning flash. We soared out into the dreary dusk.

"Let's go higher," I told the others. "Above the fog. Maybe the aliens won't be able to see us."

As the five of us climbed, the fog grew thicker, making visibility weak. We were more vulnerable than I would have liked, but then we rocketed above the murk and into a wide blue sky. It was exhilarating, like sitting on top of the world. I flew ahead and spun around, toward the heart of London. That's when exhilaration turned to fear.

"Holy ravioli," Kwan breathed.

"Are you seeing this, Ben?" Ivy asked.

"Yes. Unfortunately."

Dozens of alien ships were lurking in the dense shroud of fog over London. They were firing down into HQ. I thought about Merlin and Pellinore and Malcolm and everyone else down there who had dedicated their lives to protecting Earth.

"We have to catch 'em off guard!" I ordered. "Hit 'em hard!"

We all rocketed down at once, unleashing a storm of weapon fire, catching the aliens by surprise. Some of their ships exploded brilliantly around us. But then the aliens spotted us, and they abandoned their attack on HQ to fight back. It was five of us against almost two dozen of them.

"Try to corral them!" I shouted.

"There's too many," Darla cried back, her voice badly garbled by a faulty reception. "They keep coming!"

"Same here!" Tyler and Kwan agreed. Even through the bad reception I could hear the terror in their voices. I kept blasting alien ships out of the sky, but there seemed to be more now than there had been two minutes ago.

"There's no . . . -ay we -an stop all—!" Kwan's voice broke up as the comm system failed.

I looked up through my windshield at a layer of clouds high above. That's when I saw the ships rocketing down from the clouds. *There's something up there.*

"Can any of you still hear me?!" I bellowed. Only Ivy responded.

"Listen," I told her as I scanned the trail of aliens above me. "I have a plan. Help the others fight while I'm gone. They'll follow you!"

I blasted straight up and disappeared into the clouds. The comm system was useless now. I was all alone. Faster and faster I climbed as X-Calibur seemed to pick up speed on its own. In less than a minute I approached the edge of the atmosphere.

Looming ahead, like a dark floating mountain, was the alien mothership.

42

THE MOTHERSHIP looked like it had been constructed out of a million tons of junk, a hodgepodge of welded-together spaceships—hundreds of them, easily. It was shaped like a gigantic beehive, with the mangled and rusty ships poking out of it like thorns. I leveled out and flew closer, trying to figure out what to do next. Shooting at it would be a waste of time. By the time I could do any damage, I'd probably have fifty fighter ships attacking me.

I had to get inside it.

I veered off to go wider and circle the mothership. I was still too far away to see every nook and cranny, so I needed to get closer—a risk, but one I had to take.

Sure enough, some of the fighter ships spotted me.

"Welcome to the party," I muttered. I gave X-Calibur more power as I whisked around the ship, still looking for a way in. I soon had a line of fighter ships trailing me, with more and more aliens blasting out of the mothership like angry bees.

"Don't think. *Do*," I hissed through clenched teeth, then spun X-Calibur around and started firing at the aliens chasing me. As I unleashed all I had, I spotted a gap in the mothership's exterior up ahead, but it was too thin for X-Calibur to fit through it.

If only I could slip through that crack.

A mysterious round gauge on X-Calibur's console began pulsing, just like my countdown watch had. And, with my heart thudding in my chest, I was hit by the biggest realization of all: *The gauge was pulsing in perfect time with my heartbeat.*

"What the—" I gasped as X-Calibur's walls started to shift around me. They shimmered and softened, like liquid metal. The entire shape of the ship was *changing*, its arrow-like design transforming into a flattened disc. I remembered the X-ray Merlin showed me in his lab: Thousands of intersecting rods inside X-Calibur's walls. That skeleton was going to work now, molding the ship to become what I needed. Not what Malcolm or anyone else needed. What *I* needed. It was mind-boggling.

With the transformation complete, I soared forward. The aliens came at me, but I slipped through the crack in the mothership's exterior, leaving them in my dust. Once inside, X-Calibur began returning to its original shape.

The inside of the mothership was lined with flight bays,

stacked on top of each other like towering garages that held hundreds of fighter ships. Many of the ships were already headed toward the open panel at the front. I couldn't let them reach it.

All the buttons on X-Calibur's control console now pulsed in time with my heart. If I could get X-Calibur to change shape just by thinking it, what if I could also command its console with my thoughts? I looked to the huge open panel at the front of the mothership, trying to envision something that might stop the fighter ships from using it as a door.

Something to block them. A force field.

"Here goes nothin'." I pressed one of the buttons and kept my finger on it. That feeling of warmth I'd felt when I first touched the side of the ship days ago returned, racing up my finger, across my chest, and into my head. I gasped as I felt an indescribable rush, and X-Calibur fired.

When the blasts from X-Calibur's wings got to the open panel, they expanded outward to form a barrier across the exit, sizzling and glowing like a huge, electrified spiderweb. Some of the fighter ships that had been on their way out crashed into the barrier and exploded. Flaming debris rained down.

"THAT'S WHAT I'M TALKIN' ABOUT!!" I gave a whoop and pumped my fist in the air.

The flames from the dozen or so ships crept up the slick, oily walls and into the bays. The mothership was becoming a time bomb. I had to get out, and fast. I turned to fly back the way I had come and envisioned the ship flattening out again.

Everything was going my way—until I spotted something in the middle of the mothership coming toward me. Some*one*, about six feet tall. At first he seemed to be magically flying through the air, but as he got closer, I spotted dozens of sinewy green tentacles coming off his torso. They were hundreds of feet long and ultra thin, stretching to the mothership's walls and floor and ceiling, allowing him to bounce around the massive interior like an insect

He made a sudden lunge at me. When our eyes locked, there was no doubt in my mind who he was.

Dredmore.

43

UPON CLOSER INSPECTION, Dredmore didn't look much like a bug at all. For one thing, he had a body that resembled a human—two arms and two legs. For another, even though those weird tentacles of his were green, his skin was fleshy and gray, like a corpse. He had sharp spikes growing out of his head and back like a dinosaur, and his nose wasn't just hooked like the aliens who had invaded HQ—it was thick and wide and protruded from his elongated face like a snout. His head was huge, and his dark draconian eyes narrowed as they locked onto mine. I dug my fingers into the edges of my pilot seat and braced myself as, with a ferocious snarl, Dredmore dived straight for my windshield.

The process of changing the ship into a flattened disc again had already started. Everything around me was shimmering and gooey, so Dredmore's lunge pushed him right through X-Calibur's soft windshield. In the blink of an eye, he smashed into me with such force that the pilot seat toppled backward. The tentacles that had been connected to him unlatched from hooks on a weathered vest he wore. They hadn't been part of his body at all; they were merely an accessory. I had the vague sense that those sinewy things were *alive* as they whisked back through the windshield with multiple *TWAAANNNNG*s.

I was on my back, kicking and flailing with Dredmore on top of me. I could hear one explosion after another outside. I had to get out of there, but my mind was a mass of confusion and panic, and that had halted X-Calibur's transformation. Dredmore's breath was foul-smelling, like putrid garbage, and hot. *Really* hot. As he snarled and sneered, I could see past his razor-sharp teeth and thick, purple tongue. There was an orange glow in the back of his throat, building in intensity and heat. He had the same glow in his nostrils.

He looked me in the eye and growled, *"Ah-gankan-ruh-mana."*

I had no clue what the heck that meant, but after getting a look inside his mouth, I had a pretty good idea what was coming, so I rammed my fingers into his eyes in a last-ditch effort to get free. He roared in pain and I squirmed out from under him as a burst of *fire* shot out of his mouth and nose, missing me by inches. I scrambled backward and felt something hard hit my foot. It was Excalibur, lying on the floor. I reached for it, energized. "You want a fight—"

But as I grabbed the jeweled handle, the blade melted into a shimmering metallic puddle. It was stuck mid-transformation, just like the rest of the ship.

WHAM! Dredmore tackled me from behind, sending us both flying forward. I plunged part of the way through the windshield and dangled outside it. The heat from the fires out there was excruciating. I was going to be barbecued. I reached for the gooey nose of X-Calibur, trying to pull myself back into my ship, but there was nothing to grab onto.

"A handle," I grunted in blind agony, then envisioned it in my head. "I need a handle." Nothing happened until I pushed my hand into the silver goo. Amazingly, the goo molded itself into a handle for me.

"Thank you!" I used the handle to heave myself back through the spongy windshield and into the ship.

Inside the cabin of X-Calibur, Dredmore had gotten to his feet. He lunged at me again, but now that I had this "envisioning" thing under control, I was just getting started. I laid a hand against the shimmering wall and thought about what I wanted.

As Dredmore came at me—*BAM!* A large metallic fist, molded from the wall itself, clocked Dredmore in the side of the face. As he went down, I reached for the sword again, thinking that I needed it back to normal, and the metal of the blade quickly hardened. As Dredmore got to his feet again, I stood to face him. How fitting this was, a knight and his sword squaring off against a fire-breathing dragon.

"*Ekah-mun-haza,*" Dredmore seethed as he looked me up and down, examining me with both disdain and curiosity.

"Easy for you to say," I shot back, then swung at him.

He blasted a fireball at me and I had to dart sideways to avoid it; my swing missed. The flames clipped my legs and I fell, then went into a shoulder roll to get away from him (not an easy task while holding a massive sword). His second flame blast missed me, but one of my legs was stinging like crazy from the first one. I'd been burned, badly. I tried to limp, but went down on one knee—the pain was too much.

The mothership was probably going to detonate at any second. I stole a glance through the gooey windshield. We were almost to the back wall of the mothership, and now that I was down, Dredmore came at me again, his confidence renewed. He sucked in a big breath of air, getting ready to roast me once and for all, but I gritted my teeth against the pain of my leg and lunged, sinking my sword into his gut. The blade came out of his back.

He gasped and went to his knees as I yanked the sword out of him. His breathing was raspy and labored. Wisps of smoke drifted from his mouth and nostrils. His ability to create fire was gone; he was dying.

"Why?" I asked him through gritted teeth. "What did we ever do to you?"

He winced, holding his gut, his hands covered in a thick, purple blood. He managed a wicked grin, then looked past me, toward the windshield.

I turned. *Uh-oh.*

The mothership's wall with the crack in it was almost upon us. *Inches* away. I'd waited too long; X-Calibur wouldn't have enough time to continue flattening out. We were a second away from crashing when I realized I had any weapon I needed at my disposal.

"Something big. *Powerful*," I cried, then pressed one of the console buttons. The familiar feeling of warmth raced up my arm, chest, and head, and then—

KA-POW!! POW!! Two blasts of concentrated energy rocketed out of X-Calibur, one on each side, then came together in a split second to blow open a massive hole in the mothership. I soared through the hole and into outer space as the mothership exploded in a spectacle of monumental proportions behind me.

I grinned. I was exhausted, with my burned leg screaming, but victorious. I turned, expecting to see Dredmore's corpse on the floor.

But he was gone.

I raced over to where he had fallen only moments before and ran my hand over X-Calibur's wall. Faint splotches of purple stained the ship's interior: Dredmore's blood, mixed into the metal. He must have pushed himself out of the ship just in time.

I turned back to the windshield. Outer space was a vast sea of twinkling black that seemed to go on forever. For most it would be peaceful and serene, but not me. Not anymore. I would never look at it the same way again.

44

NOBODY IS QUITE SURE why I could bond with X-Calibur in a way that nobody else could. The techs have suggested bio-signature mumbo-jumbo, and Merlin seems to think the ship just likes me because I'm a nice guy.

In the hours following my return to HQ, there was much to be happy about. Ivy, Darla, Kwan, and Tyler had defeated the alien fighter ships. With the mothership blown into oblivion, we'd won the war, and mankind was safe—for now. Merlin, Pellinore, Malcolm, and everyone else who worked for the RTR had escaped with their lives. There'd been plenty of scrapes and bruises and concussions, but that seemed like a small price to pay, especially considering that HQ had been ninety percent destroyed. Malcolm congratulated me, but I still think he would have preferred being the one to square off against Dredmore. I also think he's a little jealous of my burned leg and limp, although they'll heal soon enough. Until then, I'll have to tolerate all the attention it's getting me (and the attention from Ivy isn't so bad).

The residents of London still aren't sure what happened in their city that day. Some claim that entire blocks were destroyed by gas leaks brought on by an earthquake. Others claim they saw something sinister in the sky, but nobody could say what. And the explosions in the sky? "Atmospheric reflections" of the explosions that were taking place on the ground. A one-in–a-million occurrence, the scientists on TV claimed. If there's one thing I learned, it's that people will believe just about *anything* before they believe that aliens exist.

Lately, I've been wondering a lot about fate and destiny. If Malcolm hadn't been knocked unconscious at the celebration party, I might not have been the one to get inside X-Calibur and finally realize what it can do. Do I believe, like Merlin does, that there are no accidents? I can't say for sure. Is there more of my life already written in the stars? More stories left to tell?

What I do know is that the RTR must rebuild. When Merlin first brought me to London, I had envisioned a time when this would be over, when I'd be able to go home and resume my average life. But I realize that's impossible now. Even if Dredmore is dead, who knows what else might be waiting to take another stab at wiping out mankind?

I can never go back to my old life now. I know too much. I've seen too much.

The thing is, I feel lucky. Some people have to wait their entire lives to find out who they're supposed to be. I'm just thirteen years old, and I already know. I'm a modern-day knight, and my mission is to protect mankind. From here on out, I plan to give that everything I've got. Because that's what Dad would do.

And you know what? I'm pretty sure he's proud of me.

ACKNOWLEDGMENTS

This book would not exist (or kick as much butt as it does!) without these amazing people. A huge thanks:

To everyone at Penguin: Pete Harris, for his awesome support from day one; Jen Besser, for getting the ball rolling and giving me much-needed encouragement right out of the gate; and Ari Lewin and Paula Sadler, for really digging in and making it happen and being cool and *nice* to me every step of the way.

To my managers at Magnet Management, for being with me on my professional writing journey since the beginning.

To a few friends who were instrumental in encouraging me over the years: Steve Sfetku, Jeff Masley, and Jim Brooks.

To Aunt Terry, Uncle Dave (I wish you were here to read this), and Aunt Maria, for always making an effort to show that family is important.

To my brother, David, for sending me an e-mail after I moved to L.A. and telling me that in the eyes of everyone back home, I had "already made it." That e-mail meant a lot to me. Rock and roll! Keep the faith!

To Julie, for the good times. The good ones weren't just good, they were great; I will never forget them.

To my parents, P.J. and Lorraine (I call them Mom and Dad), for being the best parents a son could ever have. We can't choose our parents, but I lucked out; if we could choose, I'd still choose mine. There are no words big enough to describe how much love and respect I have for them both.

And lastly, to my daughter, Abigail. Nothing is more valuable to me than knowing she'll read this book one day and understand that dreams can come true, because one of them has come true for me. My greatest wish is that she'll have the courage and determination to chase some fantastic dreams of her own.